AF583244

Acknowledgments

This journey has been an exploration of imagination, resilience, and the unwavering support of the people closest to my heart.

To my wife, **Tithi**, your love and belief in me have been the anchor of my life. Your patience, encouragement, and endless support have been a source of strength through every step of this journey. Thank you for always standing by my side and inspiring me to pursue my dreams.

To my brothers, **Sujoy** and **Pronoy**, with whom I have shared countless memories, from the joys of childhood to the trials of life. Together, we've faced thick and thin, and it's those shared moments that have shaped who I am today. Your stories, laughter, and camaraderie are woven into the very fabric of this book. Thank you for always being my pillars of support, for lifting me up when I faltered, and for reminding me of the importance of resilience and love.

To **Algo**, who has taught me so much about life, innocence, and the profound joy of living in the moment. Your companionship is a reminder of the beauty in simplicity and the power of unconditional love.

To my **family and friends**, your understanding and encouragement have been a guiding force throughout this creative journey. Thank you for your patience and for believing in me, even when the hours grew long and the nights sleepless.

To the readers, you are the reason stories are told. Thank you for stepping into this world and sharing this journey with me. I hope these pages leave an indelible mark on your heart and mind.

Lastly, to all the storytellers and dreamers, never stop weaving your tales and chasing the spark of creativity that sets your soul alight.

With all my gratitude,
Joy Mukerjee

Cover Design & Editing: Joy Mukerjee

For permission requests, please contact:
joymukerjee@icloud.com

Dedicated to my late grandfather
Mr. A.S. Mukerjee, whose wisdom, love, and
stories continue to inspire me every day.

Author's Note

Dear Reader,

Thank you for embarking on this extraordinary journey through the fragile realities of Lyra's world. When I first conceived this story, it was not meant to simply entertain or transport you to a distant realm—it was meant to challenge, to provoke thought, and perhaps, to make you question the very fabric of your own existence.

At its core, this book is a conversation—a dialogue between the characters, the narrative, and you, the reader. It's an exploration of choice, identity, and the illusions we construct to make sense of our lives. Writing it was an act of discovery for me, just as reading it is, I hope, an act of discovery for you.

There were moments during the writing process when the lines blurred for me, much as they do in the story. I would find myself wondering: Who am I writing this for? And who, exactly, is telling this story? In those moments, I realized something profound: this tale doesn't belong to me alone. It belongs to you, the one holding these pages, experiencing these words, and interpreting them in ways I can never fully anticipate.

Through Lyra's journey, I wanted to create a space where imagination and introspection collide. A story that doesn't give you all the answers but instead hands you the questions. Questions like: *If you could change your reality, would you? If everything you knew was an illusion, would it make your experiences any less real?*

This book is an invitation to look inward as much as outward. To ponder the weight of choices, the nature of time, and the profound connection between the observer and the observed. It's a story about Lyra, yes, but it's also a story about you—about all of us navigating the complexities of existence.

I also want to acknowledge the deep inspiration I drew from the boundless creativity of speculative fiction and philosophy. To those who came before me, who dared to ask the big questions and leave some unanswered, I owe an immeasurable debt.

As you close this book, I hope it leaves you with more than just memories of Lyra and her companions. I hope it leaves you with a sense of wonder, a tinge of ambiguity, and the realization that perhaps the most meaningful stories are the ones we live every day.

Thank you for letting this story become a part of your reality, if only for a little while. And thank you for being a part of its reality, for without you, this tale would simply remain an unspoken thought, lost in the void.

With infinite gratitude and curiosity,
Joy Mukerjee

Contents

Outline

In the vast expanse of existence, where stars burn and fade, where time stretches and folds, and where choices ripple endlessly, there lies a fracture—a rift that beckons not the brave nor the wise, but the willing. This tale is not a mere story etched on pages; it is an exploration, a reflection, and perhaps, a question. Not just about the world of Lyra and her companions but about you, the one who holds this narrative in their hands.

The world you are about to enter is fragile, not because it lacks strength but because it trembles on the brink of revelation. It begins as all stories do, with a moment, a catalyst—a spark that sets the wheels of destiny into motion. But unlike other tales, this one is not content to be told. It will demand your participation, your reflection, and ultimately, your confrontation with the boundaries of reality itself.

Lyra's journey begins with the ordinary: a simple life shaped by hidden truths and unexplored possibilities. Yet, beneath the surface of her existence lies something far greater. A secret, a fracture, and an unfolding truth that pulls not only her but you into its grasp. This is a story about discovery, not just of a world but of self.

As you step into Lyra's world, you will find it eerily familiar yet utterly alien. It is a realm where reality seems steadfast until it begins to bend and twist, revealing the fragility of the truths we cling to. At first, you may think yourself an observer, watching as Lyra, Korrin, Erya, and Azrin confront the mysteries before them. But soon, you will realize that the walls between you and them are far thinner than they seem.

Korrin's strength hides a broken past, and his fragmented memories hold keys to a greater mystery. Erya's mastery of arcane knowledge unravels truths that perhaps should have stayed hidden. Azrin, the scholar, peers too deeply into the abyss of forbidden knowledge, bringing back questions that cannot be answered. And then there is Lyra, a paradox in herself—a force of nature and a figure of uncertainty.

Together, they traverse landscapes both beautiful and terrifying: halls of mirrors that reflect not just what is but what could be, timelines where choices branch into infinite possibilities, and spaces where the boundaries of time and reality dissolve. You will walk these paths with them, but as you do, you will feel a weight—a pull that goes beyond the characters.

It is as if the story is not merely being told to you, but through you.

The rift that Lyra and her companions seek to understand is not just a fracture in their world. It is a mirror, reflecting every choice, every moment, and every version of themselves. These mirrors are not bound to their reality alone. They reach out, drawing you in, forcing you to confront the nature of your own decisions.

When Korrin stands before the largest mirror, his reflection flickering wildly between his past, present, and future selves, it is not just his fate he sees. It is yours. When Erya's incantations reveal the endless threads of possibility, it is not just their world that unravels—it is the fabric of your own understanding.

Through their journey, you will be asked to consider the unanswerable: *What if every decision you've ever made exists somewhere, living its own life, shaping its own world? And if so, who are you in the grand tapestry of existence?*

As the group ventures deeper into the heart of the rift, reality itself begins to unravel. Scenes repeat and shift, dialogues echo with subtle changes, and moments once familiar become strange and disjointed. It is not just their reality breaking apart—it is yours.

The characters no longer remain confined to their roles within the story. They begin to look outward, their gazes piercing the veil that separates them from you. Lyra's voice becomes sharper, her words directed not at her companions but at the unseen force that watches and shapes.

"You've been here all along, haven't you? Watching. Waiting. But why? Are you the one pulling the strings, or are you just as lost as we are?"

This is where the lines blur. Where the narrative no longer belongs solely to Lyra and her companions but to you as well. The choices you make—or refuse to make—will shape the events to come.

As the story spirals toward its climax, the rift grows wider, and the characters grow more desperate. They will ask for your guidance, not as an abstract observer but as someone who holds the power to shape their fate.

Korrin may turn to you, his voice trembling: *"If you could go back, would you? Would you undo the pain, even if it meant losing everything else?"*

Erya's eyes might pierce through you as she demands: *"Is this what you wanted? For us to question everything we are? Or are we merely pawns in a game we can't even comprehend?"*

And Lyra, always Lyra, will step closer, her presence almost tangible: *"I don't think you understand. This isn't just about us. It's about you. Why are you here? What are you trying to find?"*

Their questions will not have easy answers. They are not meant to. Instead, they will leave you questioning yourself: *What would I do if I had the power to rewrite everything? Would I choose differently? Would I risk everything for another chance?*

When the end approaches, it will not come with clarity. Instead, it will bring ambiguity, a sense of unravelling yet also of resolution. Lyra and her companions may find the answers they seek, but those answers will only lead to more questions—questions that reach out to you, entangling you in their web.

As the rift collapses, you will be faced with the ultimate paradox: *If reality is an illusion, does it matter? If observing something gives it meaning, what happens when we stop looking?*

The final moments will be haunting, beautiful, and deeply personal. You will be left with echoes of Lyra's voice, the threads of infinite possibilities, and the lingering sense that perhaps you were not just reading a story—you were living it.

This is not a tale that ends neatly. It does not close the door on its world but instead leaves it ajar, inviting you to peek through and wonder. What lies beyond the illusion? What lies beyond the choices we make, the lives we lead, and the stories we tell ourselves?

This is more than a story about Lyra and her companions. It is a story about you—about the fragile, beautiful, and mysterious nature of existence. It is an invitation to question, to reflect, and to explore.

So step into the rift. Let go of certainty. Embrace the unknown. For in the end, it is not the answers that matter but the act of questioning itself. That is where meaning is found.

The First Ripple

I've been told all my life that time is the one thing we can never truly understand. That it's this constant, steady march forward — an unstoppable, unyielding force that we can only try to keep pace with. And for most of my life, I believed it. I thought that if I just followed the rhythm of it, I would be fine. That I could measure it, plan around it, and maybe even find some semblance of control. But I was wrong. Time isn't what they told us. It's not constant. It's not even real, not in the way you think it is.

You're probably wondering how I know that. You're probably wondering who I am, and why I'm talking to you like this. Well, let me start from the beginning.

My name is Lyra, and I can sense time. Not in the way you think. It's not like I'm some oracle who can predict the future or know exactly what will happen next. No, it's more like... I feel it. Like when you stand too close to something that hums, and you can feel the vibration in your bones. I can feel time bending. The moment when everything starts to fall apart, you can't ignore it. You know it's happening, even though no one else does.

I guess that's how it all started for me — with these strange, subtle moments where I felt *something* wasn't right. You know how sometimes you think you've forgotten something important, but you can't remember what it is? It's like that, except I could feel it physically. A shift. A slight bend in reality. A faint ripple across time that most people wouldn't even notice. But I could. And it was getting worse.

At first, it was small. Nothing major. A missing object that would show up in the wrong place. A person who seemed to be in two places at once. It was easy to brush off at first. But then things started happening that I couldn't explain away. People disappearing. Whole conversations that never happened, but I was *sure* I had them. You ever have a conversation with someone, only to find out later that it never happened? Or a day that just — vanishes? It's like the universe has this tiny little hole in it, and stuff keeps slipping through, disappearing, never to be seen again.

I'm sure you're thinking I'm crazy right now. That's what everyone else thought, too. But if you're really listening, and if you're still with me, you need to know that I'm not imagining this. I'm not some delusional person talking about imaginary things. I've seen it. I've felt it. Time itself is unstable. It's tearing at the seams. And it's only getting worse.

It's not just that things are *vanishing.* It's worse than that. The more these Perennial-Rifts happen, the more I can feel the *shift.* I don't know how to explain it. It's like time itself is sick, and I can hear its pulse starting to falter. Like when a clock starts to slow down, tick by tick, and you know it's about to break. I'm not the only one who's felt it, either. People have started to notice. Objects flicker in and out of existence. People vanish, only to return, but not the same. The world has become unhinged, and no one seems to know why.

But me? I know why. Or at least, I know part of it. I've been feeling this ever since I was a child. I thought I was just imagining it then, too. But it's different now. It's bigger. I can see it. I can feel the pattern. These aren't random events. No, this is something bigger. Something ancient. And it's been getting stronger. It's like the universe is trying to forget itself, trying to break free of its own timeline. And I — I might be the only one who can stop it.

But I'm not going to lie to you — it's terrifying. Because, you see, I'm not sure if I can fix it. In fact, I'm not sure I can even survive it.

You're probably wondering what I mean by all this. What *exactly* are these "Perennial-Rifts"? Let me explain. They're moments when time, as you understand it, becomes unstable. And they're happening all over the world. You might not notice them at first — they're subtle. But trust me, they're happening. People are disappearing, whole cities are vanishing from maps, and even the smallest moments of life are being wiped from existence. It's like a glitch in reality itself.

So why are they happening? That's the million-dollar question, isn't it? I wish I could say I have all the answers, but I don't. All I know is that it's getting worse. There's a force behind it. Something ancient. Something powerful. And I've seen it — not with my eyes, but with my *mind.* I've seen the face of the thing that's causing all of this. And it's not something you can kill. It's not something you can stop in the usual ways. It's not a monster, or a person. It's *time.* Time itself is the enemy.

Now, you might be asking yourself, "How can time be the enemy? Isn't time just what we live in? It's just there. It's constant. It can't hurt us." But that's the lie they've been feeding us, isn't it? Time isn't constant. Time isn't just some invisible clock ticking away in the background of our lives. Time is *alive.* Time is a force, a thing with its own will. And it's breaking down. It's trying to tear itself apart.

I've seen it, felt it. I can sense the Perennial-Rifts before they happen. I know when they're coming, even if no one else does. That's why I'm telling you this now. Because you need to understand. You need to know that reality — the one you think is so stable, so fixed — is anything but.

And you're probably wondering: Why me? Why am I the one who can sense this? Why not someone else? And the answer is simple, but hard to hear I was born this way. I've always been attuned to the pulse of time. I can feel it in my bones, in my blood. But here's the thing: Being able to feel something isn't the same as being able to stop it.

I'm not here to give you all the answers. I can't. Because the truth is, I don't have them all myself. But what I do know is that the Perennial-Rifts are coming for us. And they're only going to get worse. The question is: Will we be ready? Will *you* be ready?

I'm telling you this now because we don't have much time. The clock is ticking, and soon, it won't matter what you think is real. Reality itself is beginning to break down. And when it does, there will be no going back.

So stick with me. Listen to me. And maybe — just maybe — we can figure this out together.

Part I-
Unravelling of Time

1

A Glimpse of Time's Collapse

The air was heavy that morning, like something was wrong, something waiting to happen. Have you ever felt it? That gnawing sensation at the edge of your consciousness, like you're standing on the brink of something you can't yet see but know will come? I had no idea what it was at first. But I felt it in my bones. It felt like time was... slipping. And I, of all people, should have known better.

I don't blame you if you're sceptical. It's hard to imagine the way time itself can go wrong, isn't it? We live in this rhythm of hours, minutes, days—a predictable cycle. So steady. So constant. And when that constant breaks, when it cracks and splinters, it's like nothing you ever thought possible. That's what I've learned. What I'm still learning.

Let me take you back to that day. The day when time showed its true face to me for the first time, its ugliness unmasked. It wasn't a loud explosion or a sudden earthquake. No, it was something far more unsettling. The world just...

staggered, like someone had hit pause and play a bit too fast.

I was standing in my favourite café, the one with the mismatched chairs and that old record player humming softly in the corner. You know, the one that smells like coffee and worn-out books. It's funny, isn't it? How something so ordinary can feel so comforting yet be so fragile in the grand scheme of things. People sipped their drinks, scrolling through their phones, chatting with friends. Everything was so... normal. That's when it happened.

There's a moment when everything blurs—a second, maybe less—and then, in that blur, people and objects just... vanished. It wasn't a full disappearance, like they were never there. No. It was more like... they flickered. One moment, I was watching the woman in the corner laugh with her friend, and the next—nothing. She was gone. But not gone in the way you'd think. No. It was like her presence had been erased, like she had never been there at all. I blinked, and there she was again, seated at the table, perfectly normal. No one else had noticed. No one except me.

I was frozen. It didn't make sense. It couldn't. How could something like that happen in the blink of an eye, and why was I the only one who saw it?

I should have turned and run, should have screamed or called for help. But I didn't. Instead, I walked out of that café and into the streets, every step heavier than the last. It wasn't just her. It was everything. It wasn't a nightmare. No. It was worse. It was like reality itself was breaking apart.

And there, right in front of me, was my first real glimpse of it: Time, not as this steady, reliable force, but as something... fragile. Something alive, pulsing and unpredictable. The world around me felt like it was warping, as though reality was being pulled in different directions at once.

But even with all that chaos swirling around me, I could still hear the sound of my own heartbeat, slow and steady, keeping rhythm like it always did. And that, I think, was the strangest thing of all. I wanted to believe it was all in my head. A stress-induced episode. Maybe I was just imagining things.

But then it happened again. And again. Each time, it became clearer: Time wasn't just fractured. It was collapsing.

I wish I could say I handled it better. But I didn't. How do you even begin to understand something like this? How do you cope when time itself starts to unravel? It wasn't just the people who vanished; it was everything—the air felt wrong, like the atmosphere had shifted ever so slightly, just enough to make me feel unbalanced. Nothing made sense.

And that's when I saw him.

He wasn't supposed to be there. Not in that place. Not in that time. His name was Owen, my older brother. He's dead, you see. He died years ago. But there he was, standing right in front of me, looking exactly as he had before. Before the accident.

I opened my mouth to speak, but no words came out. My body trembled, the world spinning around me in ways I couldn't comprehend. He looked at me, eyes wide with confusion, as if he had never left. And then... he was gone. Just like that. No warning. Nothing.

It wasn't until I turned to face the café again that I realized the truth—nothing was as it should be. Everything was changing, slipping through my fingers like sand. And I knew, deep down, that I was at the centre of it all.

But you don't understand yet, do you? The worst part wasn't that I had seen someone I loved, disappear. No, it was the fact that I could see the subtle changes. When Owen vanished, he didn't just disappear like he had before. There was something different about him when he came back—something off. A slight difference in his smile. A shift in his eyes, like he wasn't truly the person I remembered.

It's hard to explain. I'm still trying to wrap my head around it. Time, reality—it isn't what we think it is. It's not this thing that's just "there," you know? It's fragile. Easily bent. Easily broken.

Do you see it now? The paradox? The horrifying thing about time? The moment someone vanishes, and then reappears—changed. It's not a mistake. It's not an accident. It's not a trick of the mind.

I began to wonder: *Did it always happen like this?* Was time always this fragile, and I just never noticed? Or was it me? Was it because of me that things were starting to fall apart?

You probably think I'm losing my mind right now. Maybe I am. But here's the thing: I'm not the only one who's noticed. I know there are others out there like me, others who can feel it.

And you need to understand something. This isn't just about me. This is about you, too. It's about all of us. Because the truth is, if time is breaking down, then so is everything else. Reality. Existence. All of it.

What happens when time itself starts to unravel?

I guess we're going to find out together. Just... don't say I didn't warn you.

2

Mystery of Perennial-Rifts

The warmth of the café faded as soon as I stepped into the chilled air of the street. My mind buzzed, replaying every detail of the encounter with Jonas. His final words echoed louder than the bustling sounds of the city: *You don't belong in this time.*

It wasn't just the words themselves that bothered me; it was the conviction in his voice, the way he said it like he was reciting a universal truth. As if *he knew something I didn't.*

Have you ever felt like you're out of place, like the ground beneath your feet might not be as solid as you think? That's where I was. And the worst part? The feeling wasn't new. It had been simmering under my skin for as long as I could remember. Only now, it was undeniable.

I'll be honest with you: part of me wanted to run. To shove this whole thing into a box, lock it up, and throw away the key. But another part—a louder, insistent part—needed to understand. If I didn't, the uncertainty would eat me alive.

Back at my apartment, I poured over every scrap of information I could find about time anomalies. I knew Jonas' mention of "Perennial-Rifts" wasn't just a slip of the tongue. It had to mean something, but an endless loop of searches led me nowhere. Just vague theories from obscure forums and a handful of academic papers that might as well have been written in a different language.

"No one's going to hand you answers," I muttered to myself. Or maybe to you. Are you still with me? Good. Because it's about to get stranger.

As I stared at the clock on my desk, something caught my eye. The second hand twitched. Not forward, not backward—just stuck. I leaned closer, my breath fogging up the glass. Then, without warning, the hand started moving backward, erasing the last few minutes. The minute hand followed, and the hour hand too, until the clock displayed a time from hours ago.

And that's when I heard it.

My voice. Clear as day, coming from the kitchen.

"Jonas didn't just *say* it; he believed it," my voice—the other me—said. The words were exactly what I had been thinking moments ago. My heart raced as I crept toward the kitchen, every instinct screaming at me to turn back. But curiosity is a relentless thing, isn't it?

The kitchen was empty. Of course, it was. The sound had stopped as soon as I stepped through the doorway. But the feeling lingered, like the faint aftertaste of a bitter drink. I checked the clock again. It was normal now, ticking forward like nothing had happened.

You might think I'd lost my mind. Honestly, I thought so too. But that wasn't the end of it.

Over the next few days, the drifts grew more frequent. It started small: a conversation with a neighbour that I couldn't remember starting, a cup of coffee that was hot one second and cold the next. Then, bigger things. Events I knew had happened unfolding differently, like watching a film where the scenes were spliced out of order.

I tried to keep track, to make sense of it all. But how do you map something that refuses to stay still? My journal became a mess of scribbles, half-formed thoughts, and frustrated sketches of timelines that looped and overlapped. The more I tried to impose logic on the chaos, the more it resisted.

And the dreams. Have I told you about them? They weren't just dreams anymore; they were vivid, tactile experiences that clung to me long after I woke up. Sometimes, I was in the café again, but Jonas was a stranger. Other times, I'd be standing on a street corner, watching myself walk by as if I were a ghost.

One dream, though, stood out. I was sitting in my apartment, staring at the clock on my desk. The hands moved backward, faster and faster, until the face of the clock melted away, revealing... nothing. Just an empty void where time itself had ceased to exist. I woke up gasping for air, my chest tight with a dread I couldn't shake.

It wasn't until I ran into Jonas again that things started to make sense—or at least, as much sense as they could in a world that was unravelling.

"You're seeing it, aren't you?" he said, his voice low, almost a whisper. We were in the middle of a crowded park, but it felt like we were the only two people there. "The way time is breaking apart."

I nodded, too stunned to speak.

"You're not alone," he continued. "There are others. People like us."

"Like us?" I finally managed. "What does that even mean? Why is this happening?"

He hesitated, and for a moment, I saw something in his eyes that I didn't expect fear.

“Because time isn’t what we think it is,” he said. “It’s not a straight line. It’s fragile, tangled. And someone’s pulling at the threads.”

That’s where I’ll leave you for now. I know it’s frustrating, being left with more questions than answers. Trust me, I’m right there with you. But if there’s one thing I’ve learned, it’s that sometimes, you have to let the mystery breathe. Answers have a way of finding you when you least expect them.

Just do me a favour, will you? Keep an eye on the clock.

3

The Breaking Point

I'll admit, I wasn't prepared for what came next. As much as I thought I understood the Perennial-Rifts, their patterns, or lack thereof, nothing could prepare me for the sheer chaos they unleashed. It's one thing to notice a vase flickering in and out of existence or to see the hands of a clock spin backward. It's entirely another to watch a building collapse into dust, then reform as if it had never fallen, only to crumble again moments later. That day, I realized I had crossed into a realm where even my fragmented understanding of time couldn't keep up.

The Drifts had intensified. Entire streets vanished and reappeared, sometimes slightly altered, other times unrecognizable. People panicked, screaming for loved ones who were there one second and gone the next. I stood in the middle of it all, frozen, trying to process the cacophony of temporal disturbances. The world was coming apart at the seams, and I could feel the frayed edges brushing against my consciousness, like static crackling on an old TV.

"Lyra, focus," I told myself, but my words sounded hollow even to me. How could I focus when every step I took might land me in a past that no longer existed or a future I wasn't meant to see?

And then I felt it—a presence. It was faint at first, like a whisper carried on the wind, but it grew stronger, more insistent. I wasn't alone. Someone else was out there, moving through the chaos with a purpose I couldn't yet fathom.

I turned a corner and saw him—a man, older than me, with a weathered face that bore the weight of too many lost moments. He was standing in the middle of a square, his eyes closed, his hands outstretched as if feeling the air for vibrations only he could detect.

"Hey!" I called out, my voice barely carrying over the noise of reality unravelling around us. He didn't react. "Hey, can you hear me?"

He opened his eyes then, sharp and piercing, locking onto mine with an intensity that made me feel like he was looking straight through me.

"You can sense them too," he said, his voice calm despite the chaos.

I nodded, unsure how to respond. "Who are you?"

"Call me Elias," he said, lowering his hands. "And you?"

"Lyra," I replied, taking a cautious step closer. "What's happening? Why is this—" I gestured at the swirling fragments of time around us—"why is this getting worse?"

He tilted his head, studying me. "You don't know, do you?"

"Know what?" My frustration bubbled over. "I've been living with these... things, these Drifts, for months, maybe longer. I don't know what's real anymore, and now you're telling me there's something I should know?"

Elias sighed; a sound heavy with the kind of exhaustion that comes from carrying a burden too long. "It's not just happening to you. It's happening to all of us. But not everyone can see it, feel it. That makes you different. Like me."

I opened my mouth to argue, to demand answers, but then it happened again—a moment that had already happened, unfolding exactly as it had before. I saw a woman stumble over a crack in the pavement, her grocery bag spilling oranges onto the ground. I watched myself bend down to help her, only this time I wasn't actually there. I was watching it from across the square, detached yet deeply entangled.

"You're stuck," Elias said, watching my expression. "Caught in loops, reliving fragments of time that shouldn't exist. It's only going to get worse."

"Why?" I asked, my voice barely above a whisper. "Why me? Why us?"

Elias didn't answer right away. Instead, he gestured for me to follow him. "Come with me. There's something you need to see."

He led me to a place that seemed untouched by the Drifts, a quiet corner of the city where time felt... steady, if only for a moment. "This is what's left of stability," he explained. "A fragile pocket where the threads haven't frayed completely."

"Why here?" I asked, looking around. The air felt heavy, almost oppressive, but it was a welcome reprieve from the chaos.

"Because this is where it began," Elias said, his tone grave. "And where it might end."

I wanted to press him for details, but then I felt it again—that overwhelming sense of déjà vu. It wasn't just the feeling of having been in that moment before; it was the certainty that I had. The weight of it pressed down on me, suffocating, until I couldn't tell whether I was standing there in the present or reliving a memory of the same scene.

"Do we have free will?" I asked suddenly, the question bursting out of me like a dam breaking. "If we're stuck in these loops, if time is breaking down, do we even have a choice in what happens next?"

Elias looked at me, his eyes filled with a sorrow that felt all too familiar. "That's the question, isn't it?" he said. "Maybe we do. Maybe we don't. But the real question is, does it matter?"

I didn't have an answer. How could I, when nothing made sense anymore? All I knew was that the world was falling apart, and somehow, I was supposed to stop it. But as I stood there, watching time itself twist and warp around me, I couldn't shake the feeling that I was only playing out a role in a story that had already been written.

And if that was true, then who was the author?

4

The Search for the Source

Have you ever had that dream? You know the one — where you're running through an endless hallway, every door leading you back to the same spot, every turn a repeat of the last? That's what my life had become. Except I wasn't dreaming. I was trapped in a waking nightmare, where time twisted and bent around me, a cruel spiral with no way out.

Elias said it started somewhere — that there was a source. But he didn't say where or how to find it. He left me with more questions than answers, vanishing into the chaos as if he'd never been there at all. Maybe he hadn't. Maybe Elias was another paradox, another fragment of time breaking apart. Or maybe I was the one breaking. Either way, I had no choice but to keep going.

The first thing I noticed was the silence.

Not the absence of sound, but something deeper, heavier. It was as if the world itself had taken a deep breath and forgotten how to exhale. The streets were empty, the buildings eerily still. Even the air felt wrong, thick with an unseen tension that made every step feel like wading through molasses.

And then it hit me — the déjà vu.

It wasn't the usual fleeting sensation, the kind that makes you pause and wonder if you've done something before. This was stronger, sharper, like a knife pressing against my mind. Every crack in the pavement, every flicker of a streetlight, every breath I took felt achingly familiar.

Had I walked this street before?

I stopped in my tracks, the weight of the question pulling me down. I turned around, only to find myself facing the same street, the same buildings, the same cracks in the pavement. No matter which direction I looked, it was all the same. I was caught in a loop, a fragment of time playing itself out over and over again.

"Is this what it's like to lose yourself?" I whispered, my voice swallowed by the oppressive silence.

I don't know how long I wandered. Minutes, hours, days — it all blurred together, a smear of broken moments that refused to align. Somewhere along the way, I started talking to you. Not because I thought you'd answer, but because I needed to hear my own voice, to remind myself that I was still here. That I was still me.

"Do you feel it too?" I asked, looking up at the sky. It was wrong, of course. The clouds moved in jagged, unnatural patterns, like pieces of a shattered mirror trying to fit themselves back together. "The weight of it all? The sense that none of this is real?"

I laughed then, a bitter, hollow sound. "Of course you do. You wouldn't be here if you didn't."

Eventually, I found the library. Or maybe it found me. It was the only building that seemed untouched by the chaos, its doors standing wide open as if inviting me in. I hesitated at the threshold, the déjà vu crashing over me in waves. I'd been here before. I knew I had. But the memory was hazy, slipping through my fingers like sand.

Inside, the air was cold and still, the silence even heavier than outside. Rows of books stretched into the distance, their spines gleaming in the dim light. And at the centre of it all, a clock.

It was massive, its gears exposed, each one turning in precise, deliberate motions. But the hands didn't move. They hovered in place, trembling as if caught between two opposing forces.

"This is it," I murmured, stepping closer. "The source."

The clock pulsed with a strange energy, a low hum that resonated in my chest. As I reached out to touch it, the déjà vu became overwhelming, a torrent of memories and sensations flooding my mind.

I saw myself standing there, my hand hovering inches from the clock's surface. I saw myself pulling back, fear etched across my face. And then I saw something else — a version of me reaching out, defying the fear, pressing my hand against the cold metal.

Which one was real? Which one was me?

"Free will," I whispered, the words trembling on my lips. "Do I have it? Or am I just playing out a script?"

The hum grew louder, the gears spinning faster, the air crackling with electricity. I had to choose. I had to decide. But how could I, when every choice felt predetermined, every path already walked?

I pressed my hand against the clock.

The world shattered.

It wasn't like the Drifts. It wasn't fragments or flickers or loops. It was everything, all at once — every moment I'd ever lived, every decision I'd ever made, every version of me that had ever existed, colliding in a blinding explosion of light and sound.

I saw myself as a child, running through the fields behind my house. I saw myself as a teenager, staring at the stars, wondering what my future would hold. I saw myself in the present, caught in the chaos of the Drifts, struggling to hold onto what little sense of reality I had left.

And then I saw something else.

I saw the threads.

They stretched out in every direction, glowing faintly, connecting moments and memories and choices. Some were frayed, others severed entirely, but they all led back to the clock.

To me.

When I woke up, the library was gone. So was the clock. I was lying on the pavement, the world around me eerily quiet. But it wasn't the same silence as before. This was different, lighter, almost peaceful.

I sat up, my head spinning, my mind racing with questions I didn't know how to answer. Had I stopped the Drifts? Or had I simply shifted to another fragment of time, another version of reality?

"Are you still with me?" I asked, my voice trembling. "Did we... did we do it?"

I don't know if you'll answer. Maybe you're as lost as I am. But if you're still here, if you're still listening... thank you.

I don't know what happens next. But I think I'm ready to find out.

5

The First Great Paradox

Have you ever looked into a mirror and felt that the reflection, wasn't you? That something about it was... wrong? It wasn't just your face, but the way it stared back, as if it knew something you didn't. That's how it felt when I saw her.

Me. But not me.

The version of me standing in the shadows across the room wasn't just older. She was harder, her expression colder, her eyes haunted by truths I hadn't yet faced. She didn't flinch when I gasped, didn't blink when I instinctively stepped back.

"Who are you?" I managed to whisper, even though I already knew.

She smiled faintly, a smile that wasn't mine. "Isn't it obvious?"

It started with the clock. Or maybe it didn't. Maybe the clock was just another thread in the web, another piece of the puzzle I was only beginning to understand. But when I touched it

— when I made that choice — something shifted. Something broke.

And now, here she was. My future self. The version of me that had lived through the chaos, seen the threads unravelling, and somehow survived.

"Survived?" she said, her voice sharp and clipped, as if she could hear my thoughts. "Is that what you think this is? Survival?"

I blinked. "You... can hear me?"

"No," she said, stepping closer. "But I know what you're thinking. I've been you, remember?"

The words sent a chill down my spine. It wasn't just what she said — it was the way she said it, as if the very act of remembering was painful.

"What do you want?" I asked, my voice trembling.

She stopped, her gaze locking onto mine. "To warn you. To stop you."

"From what?"

"From becoming me."

The paradox was overwhelming. How could I become her if she was already here, warning me not to? How could she warn me about a choice I hadn't yet made? The questions piled up, each one heavier than the last, until I thought I might collapse under their weight.

She must have seen it in my face because her expression softened — just for a moment. “I know it’s a lot,” she said quietly. “It was for me too.”

“Then why—” I stopped, the words catching in my throat. “Why are you here?”

“Because you need to know the truth,” she said. “About the Drifts. About the threads. About why this is happening.”

She didn’t tell me everything. Of course, she didn’t. That would have been too easy. Instead, she gave me fragments, pieces of a story that only raised more questions.

“There’s a force,” she said, pacing the room like a caged animal. “A group, an organization — whatever you want to call it. They’re manipulating time, bending it to their will. The Drifts are their doing, but they didn’t start them.”

“What do you mean?”

She stopped, her eyes boring into mine. “They’re trying to fix something. Something you broke.”

The words hit me like a physical blow. “Me? How could I—”

"I don't know how," she said, cutting me off. "Not yet. But it's tied to you. To us. And if we don't stop them, the threads will snap."

I frowned. "The threads?"

She gestured around us. "Reality. Time. Space. Everything is connected, held together by threads. The Drifts are pulling them apart. And when they break..." She didn't finish the sentence, but she didn't need to. I could see the answer in her eyes.

It wasn't just what she said that unnerved me. It was the way she said it — like someone who had already lost everything. Someone who had fought and failed and was now trying, desperately, to change the outcome.

"What happens if I don't listen?" I asked.

She hesitated, her jaw tightening. "You'll find out."

It wasn't an answer, not really. But it was enough to send a shiver down my spine.

After she left — or vanished, or dissolved, or whatever it was she did — I was alone again. But the room didn't feel empty. It felt heavy, as if her presence lingered in the air, a reminder of the choices I hadn't yet made.

I sat down, my head in my hands, trying to make sense of it all. The Drifts, the threads, the organization, the future me... it was too much. Too big. How could I possibly stop something I didn't even understand?

"Are you still with me?" I whispered, hoping you were. "Because I don't think I can do this alone."

The first clue came the next morning. Or maybe it wasn't morning. Time didn't work the way it should anymore, and the light streaming through the windows felt off, too bright and too dim all at once.

The letter was on the table, a single sheet of paper folded neatly in half. There was no name, no address, no sign of who had left it. Just two words scrawled in a handwriting I didn't recognize.

Find Eden.

Eden. The name tugged at something in the back of my mind, a memory just out of reach. I turned the letter over, searching for more, but it was blank. Whoever had left it wanted me to figure it out on my own.

But how could I, when I didn't even know where to start?

The answer, it turned out, was in the threads.

I didn't see them all the time, but when I focused — really focused — they began to appear. Fine, glowing lines stretching out in every direction, connecting moments and places and people. Some were tangled, others frayed, but they all pulsed with a strange, otherworldly energy.

I followed one, then another, letting the threads guide me. They led me through empty streets and crumbling buildings, through places that felt both familiar and alien. And then, finally, they led me to Eden.

It wasn't a person. It wasn't even a place, not really. It was a machine — massive and complex, its gears and wires humming with power.

And at its centre was a clock.

I stared at it, my heart pounding in my chest. This was it. The source, the cause, the answer to everything.

Or maybe it was just the beginning.

Part II-
Temporal Turmoil

6

Time Collapsing Inwards

Do you ever feel like the world is unravelling one thread at a time?
I do now. Not just in the poetic, existential way most people mean. No, I mean literally. Time—the glue that holds reality together—is tearing apart. And me? I'm the one stuck trying to piece it back together, or at least figure out why it's falling apart in the first place.

Since leaving Eden, the sense of displacement hasn't left me. Time feels...wrong. It's hard to explain, but I'll try. Imagine standing in a hallway filled with mirrors. You can see your reflection endlessly, but only one version is *you.* Now imagine that some reflections move out of sync—or worse, move before you do. That's what it feels like. Except it's not just mirrors; it's the world. People, moments, places—all flickering in and out of alignment.

I noticed the first fracture while sitting at a café—a moment so mundane it felt absurd that it would become pivotal. I was watching a couple argue two tables away. They looked like they'd been together for years, the kind of couple who could fight without fear of breaking. Then, out of nowhere, they froze.

Not figuratively. Literally. They stopped moving mid-argument. The woman's hand was mid-gesture, her lips frozen in the middle of a word. The man stared back at her, unblinking. At first, I thought I was imagining it. But then it happened again.

The barista dropped a cup, and the crash echoed through the room. The sound lingered, stretching unnaturally, and the couple blinked back into motion as if nothing had happened. Except they weren't arguing anymore.

"Did you see that?" I whispered to a stranger sitting nearby.

She looked at me, confused. "See what?"

These glitches grew more frequent over the next few days. People forgetting conversations we'd just had. A bird flying backwards for a split second. My own memories splintering, as if pieces were being rewritten without my consent.

Then came the conversation that changed everything.

It was late evening, the sky painted in hues of violet and gold. I was walking through the city, trying to clear my head, when I heard a voice call my name.

“Lyra.”

I froze. The voice was unfamiliar but carried an unsettling familiarity—like a song you don’t remember learning but somehow know all the words to.

I turned to see a man standing under a flickering streetlamp. He was tall, with sharp features and an air of quiet authority. His clothes were strange, futuristic yet worn, as if they’d travelled too far through time.

“You don’t know me yet,” he said, “but you will.”

"That’s...not reassuring,” I replied, crossing my arms. “Who are you?”

He smiled faintly. “You’ll call me Ash. I’ve been waiting for this moment for a long time. Well, for me, it’s been a long time. For you...it’s complicated.”

“Try me.”

Ash sighed, running a hand through his dark hair. “I’m from your future. Or a version of it. Time is fracturing, Lyra. I think you know that already. What you don’t know is that you’re at the centre of it.”

I blinked, my stomach dropping. "Why me? What did I do?"

"It's not what you did," he said, his tone heavy with meaning. "It's what you will do."

My head spun. The conversation felt unreal, like a dream I couldn't wake up from. I wanted to demand answers, to shake him until he explained everything, but something about his expression stopped me.

"Listen," he continued, stepping closer. "Every moment you exist, time bends around you. The Perennial-Rifts aren't random; they're drawn to you. And the more they occur, the closer we get to...collapse."

"Collapse?" My voice cracked.

He hesitated before answering. "Imagine time folding in on itself, like a piece of paper crumpled into nothing. No past, no future. Just...nothing."

I wanted to laugh, to tell him he was insane, but deep down, I knew he was right. I'd seen too much—felt too much—to dismiss his words.

"What am I supposed to do?" I asked finally, my voice barely above a whisper.

Ash's expression softened, almost apologetic. "That's the thing, Lyra. I don't know. My timeline...it's already gone. I'm here because you're my only chance to fix this. But fixing it might mean sacrificing everything."

He reached into his pocket and handed me a small device—something sleek and metallic, pulsing faintly with light.

"What is this?"

"A stabilizer," he explained. "It might help you control the Drifts. Or it might make things worse. Either way, it's better in your hands than mine."

Before I could respond, the streetlamp flickered again, and Ash began to fade, his form dissolving like smoke caught in the wind.

"Wait!" I shouted. "I have more questions!"

His voice echoed faintly as he disappeared. "You'll find the answers...if you survive."

The stabilizer felt heavy in my hand, a weight that wasn't just physical. As I stared at it, a memory—one that didn't feel like mine—flashed through my mind: me, standing in a void, using the device to stop time itself.

I dropped it instinctively, my heart racing. What was happening to me?

I turned to you, the only one I can trust with this madness. **What would you do if you were me? Would you try to save time, even if it**

meant losing yourself? Or would you walk away, let someone else bear the burden?

Because I don't know how much longer I can hold on.

And that was the beginning of the end. Or maybe it was just the beginning. I'm not even sure anymore. But if you're still with me, I'll tell you what happened next.

7

Shifting Realities

I once thought time was a straight line. You know, the kind of line they show you in school, where the past stretches behind you and the future unravels ahead. Turns out, that's a lie. Time isn't a line. It's more like a kaleidoscope—fractured, chaotic, and spinning uncontrollably.

I don't know when I crossed into this place. One moment, I was holding the stabilizer Ash gave me, wondering what the hell I was supposed to do with it. The next, the world shifted. The air felt thinner, the colours sharper, and the edges of reality...blurred.

The city I stumbled into wasn't like anything I'd ever seen. It shimmered, as though it existed halfway between a dream and waking life. Buildings stood at impossible angles, their reflections stretching into infinity in rivers that ran backward. The sky was split—half-day, half-night—with stars flickering in and out of existence.

It wasn't empty, though. People moved through the streets, but they didn't seem *real.* Some flickered like old film reels, their movements jittery and out of sync. Others were duplicates of each other, like a glitch that had copied and pasted them into the same moment.

I should have been terrified. Maybe I was. But mostly, I was curious.

A figure approached me—a woman, older, with silver hair pulled into a tight braid. Her eyes were sharp, piercing, and she moved with a confidence that seemed untouched by the chaos around her.

"Lyra," she said, as if we'd met before.

"How do you know my name?"

She smiled faintly. "It's my job to know. Welcome to Chronopolis, the city outside time."

Chronopolis. Even the name felt like it didn't belong, like it had been plucked from a story too grand to be true.

"I don't understand," I said, gripping the stabilizer tightly. "What is this place?"

"Call it a nexus," the woman said. "A convergence of timelines. This is where the Perennial-Rifts are strongest. Where the fractures begin."

"Fractures," I repeated, the word heavy on my tongue. "You mean...the glitches? The things I've been seeing?"

She nodded. "They're ripples. And they're getting worse. That's why you're here."

I wanted to argue, to demand answers, but before I could, she turned and started walking. "Come. There's someone you need to meet."

She led me through the twisting streets, past buildings that seemed to breathe and alleys that looped back on themselves. Finally, we stopped in front of a structure that looked ancient, its walls etched with symbols I couldn't read.

Inside, the air was thick, heavy with the scent of old paper and something metallic. A man sat at a table covered in maps and strange devices. He looked up as we entered, and for a moment, I felt like I was staring at a mirror.

"Lyra," he said, his voice tinged with an emotion I couldn't place. "It's about time."

The woman left us, her footsteps fading into silence. I approached the table cautiously.

"Who are you?" I asked.

The man smiled sadly. "Someone who's been trying to fix this for a long time. Someone who's made...mistakes."

It took me a moment to piece it together. "You're me. Aren't you?"

He nodded. "A version of you, yes. From a timeline where I—where we—failed."

I sat down, my mind reeling. "Failed at what?"

"At stopping the collapse," he said. "The Perennial-Rifts, the fractures—they're not just anomalies. They're warnings. Time is unraveling, and it's up to you to stop it."

"How?" I demanded. "What am I supposed to do?"

He gestured to the stabilizer. "That device can stabilize small Drifts, but it won't fix the core problem. To do that, you'll have to make a choice."

Before I could ask what he meant, the room shifted. The walls rippled like water, and suddenly, we were outside, standing in the middle of a busy street.

A crowd had gathered, their faces tense. In the center of the commotion, a young boy stood frozen, his figure flickering like a faulty hologram.

"What's happening to him?" I asked.

"He's caught in a paradox," my future self explained. "If he's not stabilized, he'll slip into oblivion. But if you save him..." He hesitated.

"If I save him, what?"

"You might anchor the paradox in place, making it permanent. The Drifts could become irreversible."

The crowd grew restless, their whispers merging into a cacophony. The boy's mother, tears streaming down her face, pleaded with me. "Please, help him!"

I turned to you, my only constant in this madness. **What would you do? Save the boy, knowing it might doom us all? Or let him go, sacrificing one life for the chance to save countless others?**

I made my decision. The stabilizer felt cold in my hand as I activated it, its light casting sharp shadows across the street.

For a moment, everything froze. The boy's flickering stopped, and he looked at me with wide, terrified eyes. Then the world snapped back into motion, and he was whole again.

The crowd erupted into cheers, but I couldn't celebrate. My future self watched me with an expression I couldn't read.

"You've made your choice," he said quietly. "Now we'll see what it costs."

As the crowd dispersed, I felt the weight of the stabilizer in my hand, heavier than ever. Somewhere in the distance, the air shimmered, a new fracture forming.

Time wasn't done with me yet. And I wasn't sure if I'd made the right choice.

8

Temporal Labyrinth

The heart of the rift was nothing like I had imagined. You'd think that a place where time itself unravelled would be filled with chaos—a cacophony of moments colliding, flashes of blinding light, and the sound of universes breaking apart. But it wasn't. It was eerily quiet.

The air shimmered, not with heat but with something else entirely—a distortion, as though reality itself was holding its breath. Each step I took sent ripples through the ground, but they didn't spread outward like normal ripples. They twisted back on themselves, forming loops before fading into nothingness.

I know you're wondering what it felt like, being here. Honestly? It felt like I didn't belong, like I was a smudge on the pristine fabric of time. And yet, somehow, I knew this was exactly where I was supposed to be.

The path led me to what could only be described as a doorway. It wasn't a door in the traditional sense—no hinges, no handle. It was more like a tear in the fabric of reality, edges frayed and glowing faintly.

I hesitated. You'd think I'd be used to strange things by now, but this... this was different. Stepping through felt like crossing an invisible threshold, like the moment when you wake up from a dream but aren't sure if you're still dreaming.

And then I was inside.

The labyrinth stretched out before me, an endless series of corridors made of shifting light and shadow. Walls pulsed with an almost organic rhythm, as if the place itself was alive. Each turn seemed to lead back to where I had just been, and yet, I knew I hadn't been there before.

"Lyra," a voice echoed.

I froze. It wasn't just any voice. It was mine.

The first time it happened, I didn't realize it was a loop. I found myself standing at a junction, three paths diverging in different directions. One was bathed in golden light, another in deep shadow, and the third shimmered with a silvery glow.

Instinct took over, and I chose the golden path.

I walked for what felt like hours, though it could have been seconds. The corridor twisted and turned, leading me to a circular room with a pedestal at its centre. On the pedestal was an hourglass, its sand frozen mid-fall.

Without thinking, I reached out to touch it. The moment my fingers brushed the glass, the world shifted.

I was back at the junction.

"Lyra," my voice echoed again.

This time, I noticed the subtle differences. The golden path was no longer golden; it was tinged with red, as though stained with blood. The shadowy path seemed darker, almost suffocating. The silvery path sparkled more brightly, like stars in the night sky.

I chose the silvery path.

It didn't matter what path I chose. Every time, I ended up back at the junction. Sometimes the room with the pedestal held the hourglass; other times, it was empty. Once, I found a mirror instead, and in its reflection, I saw a version of myself I didn't recognize—older, wearier, with eyes that seemed to hold the weight of eternity.

"Why are you doing this to me?" I shouted into the emptiness.

The labyrinth didn't answer, but I felt its presence, like an unseen observer watching, waiting.

And then I started to notice something.

Each loop wasn't just a repetition. It was a new reality, a self-contained universe born from my choices. In one loop, I chose the golden path and found myself in a lush forest where time flowed backward. In another, I took the shadowy path and ended up in a desolate wasteland where time didn't exist at all.

But no matter what I did, the outcome was always the same: I returned to the junction.

Do you know what it feels like to realize that nothing you do matters? That no choice, no action, no decision will ever change the outcome? It's... suffocating.

After what felt like the hundredth loop, I stopped trying to choose. I sat down at the junction, staring at the three paths, waiting for something—anything—to change.

And then, for the first time, someone appeared.

She stepped out of the silvery path, her movements fluid and graceful, as though she belonged here. Her face was familiar in a way that made my stomach twist.

It was me.

But not me.

"Finally," she said, her voice calm but laced with a weariness I recognized all too well. "I've been waiting for you."

"Who are you?" I asked, though I already knew the answer.

"I'm you," she said. "Or rather, I'm what you'll become if you keep going."

Her words hit me like a punch to the gut.

"Why am I here?" I demanded. "What is this place?"

"The labyrinth isn't a place," she said. "It's a test. A crucible. Every decision you make here creates a new reality, but none of them matter because the labyrinth isn't about finding the right path. It's about understanding that there is no right path."

Her words echoed in my mind, unravelling something deep within me. If every choice created a new universe, then every universe was equally valid. Equally meaningless.

"What do I do?" I asked, my voice barely above a whisper.

She smiled, a sad, knowing smile. "That's the paradox, Lyra. You already know what to do. You've always known."

And then she was gone, fading into the shimmering walls of the labyrinth.

I stood at the junction, staring at the three paths. For the first time, I didn't feel fear or frustration. I felt... acceptance.

I took a deep breath and stepped forward.

Not onto the golden path. Not into the shadowy path. Not toward the silvery glow.

I stepped into the empty space between them.

And the world shattered.

9

Breaking the Cycle

When the world shattered, I expected pain, chaos, something to mark the end of the labyrinth's endless loop. Instead, there was silence—a deep, consuming stillness that wrapped around me like a cocoon. I felt weightless, untethered from everything.

Then the stillness broke.

It started as a low hum, like the resonance of a distant memory vibrating through the fabric of reality. The shards of the labyrinth reassembled themselves, not into walls or corridors, but into something far more surreal: an endless expanse of light and shadow, coexisting in perfect contradiction.

And in the centre of it all, there was a figure.

You'd think I'd be used to strange beings by now, but this one... this one was different. It didn't have a form, not really. One moment it was a towering silhouette, the next a shifting cascade of stars, and then... then it was me.

Or, at least, it wore my face.

"You've come far, Lyra," the being said, its voice reverberating through the expanse. It wasn't just speaking to me; it was speaking through me, its words resonating in my very bones.

"Who are you?" I demanded, though I wasn't sure if I wanted the answer.

"I am everything," it said simply. "And nothing. I am the paradox you seek to unravel."

My heart sank. "You're the cause of the Perennial-Rifts."

It tilted its head—or maybe I did. The line between us blurred with every passing second. "And so are you."

The words hit me like a blow. "What are you talking about?" I said, my voice shaking.

"You are both the catalyst and the cure," the being explained. "Your existence is a fracture in time, a ripple that has grown into a tidal wave. Without you, the rift would not exist. But without you, it cannot be mended."

I wanted to deny it, to push back against the crushing weight of its words, but deep down, I knew it was telling the truth. I had always felt out of place, like I didn't quite belong—not in the normal flow of time, anyway.

"You're lying," I whispered, but the conviction in my voice wavered.

"Am I?" it asked, and suddenly the expanse shifted.

Images surrounded me—snapshots of my life, moments frozen in time. There I was as a child, staring in awe at a clock that seemed to tick backward. There I was at the first rift, my hands trembling as I reached into its glowing core. And there I was, countless times over, making choices, causing ripples, unravelling time without even realizing it.

But the most gut-wrenching image was the last: me, standing in this very place, my hand outstretched toward the being.

This wasn't the first time I had been here.

"Every loop brings you back to this moment," the being said. "Every time, you face the same decision. And every time, you choose."

"What decision?" I asked, though I already knew.

"To end it," it said. "To cease existing and reset time, erasing yourself from all history. Or to let the paradox persist, knowing it will continue to unravel reality."

The weight of its words settled on me like a crushing tide. If I chose to erase myself, it wouldn't just be my future that disappeared. Every memory, every interaction, every moment where I had touched someone's life—it would all vanish.

I thought of you then. Yes, you. Don't think I haven't noticed you here, following my journey, witnessing my every step. You've been with me through it all, haven't you? And now... now I have to decide if I'll let you go, too.

"What happens if I let the paradox persist?" I asked, my voice barely a whisper.

"The rift will grow," the being said. "Time will collapse further. Reality itself will unravel, piece by piece."

"And if I erase myself?"

"The rift will close. Time will heal. But you will cease to exist. Every version of you, every trace, gone."

I swallowed hard. The choice was impossible. How do you weigh the fate of an entire universe against your own existence?

The being stretched out its hand—my hand—and in its palm was a fragment of the labyrinth, glowing faintly.

"This is your moment, Lyra," it said. "Choose."

I hesitated, my mind racing. Could I really do it? Could I erase myself, knowing that it would save everyone else? Or was I selfish enough to cling to my existence, even if it meant condemning reality to collapse?

I turned to you then. Yes, you. What would you do if you were in my place? Would you sacrifice everything for the greater good? Or would you hold on, hoping that somehow, some way, there was another solution?

I wish I could say that your presence gave me clarity, but the truth is, the choice was mine alone. It always had been.

With trembling fingers, I reached out and took the fragment from the being's hand. The moment I did, the expanse began to ripple, reality bending and twisting around me.

"Goodbye," I whispered, not just to the being, but to you.

And then I made my choice.

9

The End or the Beginning

When I made my choice, I thought it would be simple. Isn't that funny? After everything I've been through, I still clung to the naive belief that the end could be clean. That one decision could tie everything up, neatly and completely.

But, as you probably guessed, time doesn't work that way.

The moment I placed the fragment into the fabric of reality, the world... shifted. Not in the way the labyrinth did, with its dizzying loops and subtle distortions, but in a way that felt final. Time shuddered, like the first crack in a dam, and then burst wide open.

I expected pain—searing, cosmic, all-encompassing—but it wasn't like that. What I felt instead was *absence*.

Imagine standing in a crowded room, surrounded by the buzz of voices and movement, and then, in an instant, everything falls silent. It's not peaceful or calming; it's suffocating. That's what it felt like as my essence began to unravel. Memories slipped through my grasp like water, moments fading before I could cling to them.

Each thread of my being dissolved into the void, and yet, I was aware of every fragment that left me. Every laugh, every tear, every step of this journey—gone.

And still, I lingered.

The rift that had threatened to consume everything was closing, its jagged edges smoothing out, sealing itself with the energy of my sacrifice. I should have felt relief, satisfaction even, but instead, there was a nagging unease—a faint vibration at the edge of perception.

Then I saw it.

Where I had been—where *I* should no longer be—a pinpoint of light emerged. It was small at first, almost imperceptible, but it pulsed with a rhythm that felt... familiar.

The light expanded, growing in size and intensity, until it filled the space I had left behind. It wasn't just light; it was *me*, or at least something that remembered being me.

"That's not supposed to happen," I whispered, though there was no one to hear.

And then it hit me: my absence hadn't stabilized the timeline. It had destabilized it further.

Before I could process what was happening, a voice echoed through the void. It wasn't the being I had confronted, nor was it my own. It was something deeper, resonating from the very fabric of existence.

"Lyra," the voice said, and it carried a warmth that was both comforting and alien. "You have seen the truth of time. Now, you must understand its nature."

"Understand?" I echoed, my voice trembling. "I gave everything. What more is there to understand?"

The light pulsed, and with it came a surge of memories—not just mine, but fragments of countless timelines, countless versions of reality.

"You believe your choice was an end," the voice continued. "But time has no end, no beginning. It is a river, ever flowing, ever changing. And you, Lyra, are its current."

The light around me shifted, and suddenly, I wasn't in the void anymore. I stood on a vast, shimmering plain, where the ground was made of fractured mirrors reflecting endless skies. Each fragment showed a different version of reality: some where the rift had consumed everything, others where it had never existed at all.

"You are both the cause and the effect," the voice said. "The spark that ignites the flame and the ashes it leaves behind. This is the paradox of your existence."

I stared at the reflections, each one more surreal than the last. In one, I saw myself standing in a bustling city, laughing with strangers. In another, I was alone in the ruins of a world long dead.

"Why show me this?" I asked, my voice breaking. "What am I supposed to do?"

"Choose," the voice said simply.

I laughed bitterly. "You're asking me to *choose*? After everything, after I've already given everything, you still want more?"

The mirrors trembled, the reflections rippling like water.

"Every choice creates a new reality," the voice said. "Every action, a new iteration. You believed your sacrifice would end the cycle, but it has only begun anew. The question is not whether you will act, but how."

I fell to my knees, staring at my fractured reflection. "What's the point? If every choice leads to the same end, why does it matter?"

"Because" the voice said, soft but firm, "it is not the end that defines you. It is the journey."

The light grew brighter, enveloping me in its warmth. Memories surged through me again, but this time, they weren't just mine. They were the memories of every version of me, every path I had taken, every choice I had made.

I saw myself as a child, wide-eyed and curious, dreaming of the stars. I saw myself standing at the edge of the rift, terrified but determined. I saw myself as something greater, something beyond human, a being of pure energy and will.

And in that moment, I understood.

Time wasn't broken. It wasn't something to be fixed. It was alive, fluid, infinite. And I was a part of it—not its master, not its prisoner, but its heart.

I turned then, not to the voice, but to you.

"You're still here," I said, my voice trembling. "After everything, you stayed."

I smiled, though tears streamed down my face. "I don't know what's coming next. I don't even know if I'll still be... *me*. But if you're willing, I'd like you to come with me. Just a little further."

The light pulsed, and I felt its warmth enveloping both of us.

"Shall we?"

As the light carried me forward, the shimmering plain dissolved into a kaleidoscope of colours and shapes. The mirrors shattered, their fragments swirling around me like stars.

And then, slowly, a new world began to take shape—a world unlike any I had ever seen.

This wasn't the end. It was never the end. It was only the beginning.

So, are you ready? Because I am.

Part III-
The Aftermath

11

Fragments of a Forgotten World

The first thing Korrin noticed about the new reality was the quiet. Not the comforting silence of a peaceful dawn, but the kind of quiet that echoed like a question no one dared to answer.

The world wasn't as it should be.

Korrin had spent years studying anomalies, the inexplicable cracks in the fabric of existence that seemed to defy all reason. Yet this was different. The air was thick with the remnants of something—or someone—who had been wiped clean from the universe. A faint, unshakable impression lingered, like the shadow of a memory too stubborn to fade.

"Do you feel it too?" Korrin whispered, as if speaking too loudly might shatter the fragile balance of this place.

But there was no one to answer.

The timeline had stabilized—or so it seemed. Across the vast expanse of existence, life continued as it always had. People went about their routines, oblivious to the seismic shift that had just occurred. And yet, something was undeniably missing.

You might be wondering, reader, who I am. I suppose I should have introduced myself earlier, but I'm not entirely sure how to explain it. Perhaps it's better if I show you.

Korrin was not from this timeline. They were a seeker, one of the few beings capable of navigating the ever-shifting tapestry of reality. They had seen timelines collapse and rebuild, universes born and destroyed. But never had they encountered a world like this one.

There were traces—fragments, really—scattered like breadcrumbs across time and space. A faint echo in the fabric of the universe, whispering a name that no one else seemed to know.

Lyra.

It started with a simple anomaly. Korrin had been tracking rift activity when they stumbled upon a peculiar distortion in a forgotten corner of time. A shard of glass suspended midair, its surface rippling with an unearthly light.

As Korrin reached out to touch it, the shard flickered, and for a brief moment, an image appeared—a woman with dark, stormy eyes and an expression caught between determination and sorrow.

She turned to look at Korrin, as if she could see them through the veil of existence.

“Who are you?” Korrin murmured, their voice trembling.

The shard dissolved into nothingness, leaving behind only an ache, a longing that Korrin couldn’t explain.

“Lyra,” the name slipped from their lips unbidden.

It wasn’t just a name. It was a feeling, a presence, as if the universe itself was holding its breath, waiting for her return.

Korrin began piecing together the fragments, each one more haunting than the last. A melody drifting through a deserted timeline, its notes echoing with a bittersweet familiarity. A sketch etched into the walls of a collapsing reality, depicting a woman standing on the edge of an endless void.

The fragments were scattered across dimensions, each one telling a story of someone who should not exist—someone who had been erased.

And yet, dear reader, I suspect you’ve felt it too, haven’t you? That gnawing sense of loss, that quiet voice at the back of your mind whispering a name you can't quite remember.

Lyra was gone, but her absence was louder than any presence could ever be.

As Korrin gathered the fragments, a pattern began to emerge. Each piece resonated with the others, forming a mosaic that defied the laws of time and space. Slowly, a ghostly image of Lyra began to take shape, flickering like a candle in the wind.

"Why do you haunt me?" Korrin asked the image one night, their voice cracking under the weight of unspoken questions.

The image did not answer, but in its silence, Korrin felt a strange sense of understanding. Lyra wasn't haunting them. She was trying to guide them.

But to what end?

You might think, dear reader, that Korrin's journey is one of discovery. And you wouldn't be wrong. But it's also a journey of connection—of understanding what it means to exist in a world where someone like Lyra could leave such an indelible mark.

Perhaps you've felt it too, that sense of being pulled toward something greater than yourself. Perhaps you've wondered if your choices matter, or if you're simply a fragment in someone else's story.

Korrin wondered the same thing.

The search led Korrin to the heart of the anomaly—a place where time stood still, and the boundaries between realities blurred into a kaleidoscope of possibilities.

There, suspended in the void, was the final fragment: a crystalline structure pulsing with an otherworldly light.

As Korrin approached, the structure began to hum, resonating with a frequency that seemed to speak directly to their soul.

And then, for the briefest of moments, Korrin saw her. Lyra, standing at the edge of eternity, her eyes filled with a quiet determination.

"I am the fragment," her voice echoed, as if carried on the winds of time. "And so are you."

The crystalline structure shattered, and the world around Korrin dissolved into a blinding light.

When the light faded, Korrin was alone. The fragments were gone, and with them, the image of Lyra.

But something had changed.

The universe no longer felt empty. It was as if Lyra's absence had been replaced by a quiet promise—a reminder that even in the face of erasure, traces of existence could endure.

And so, dear reader, the question remains: How can someone who never existed leave such a profound mark on reality?

Perhaps it's not about existence at all. Perhaps it's about the stories we tell, the connections we make, and the fragments we leave behind.

Korrin didn't have the answers. But they knew one thing for certain: the search was far from over.

And maybe, just maybe, Lyra's story wasn't finished yet.

12

The Rift Reimagined

Korrin's journal entry crackled faintly under the glow of a lantern. The pages, though worn and delicate, seemed oddly warm in his hands—a side effect, perhaps, of the residual energy he'd encountered near the latest anomaly. His pen hovered above the parchment as if hesitating to commit his thoughts.

"An anomaly that breathes, that shifts...is it alive?" Korrin scrawled the words hastily, the ink bleeding slightly at the edges of the letters. He could feel the hum of something greater than himself, vibrating just out of reach.

The Rift, as it was known by those few aware of its existence, had evolved. It no longer tore silently through the fabric of time; it now shimmered, pulsating faintly, as though inhaling and exhaling the essence of existence itself. The air around it felt denser, like wading through an unseen tide, and it whispered—soft, fragmented words, half-lost in their journey to coherence.

This time, the whisper came clear.

"You seek...her."

Korrin froze. The lantern light flickered, shadows dancing across his face. The voice wasn't external; it resonated inside his mind, reverberating like an echo that didn't belong.

"Who is *her*?" Korrin muttered, though no one was there to hear him.

The Rift pulsed in response, ripples cascading across its surface like the shimmer of water under moonlight.

The Rift wasn't an entity that could be seen completely; it occupied spaces between dimensions, where even understanding became fractured. Korrin knelt before it, observing the way it seemed to observe him in return.

"You're alive," he whispered, the words slipping out before he could stop them.

A tendril of energy curled toward him, like a flicker of sentience reaching out for acknowledgment. This time, he didn't flinch.

"You...were her," the Rift whispered again, its voice layered with tones of grief, longing, and something else Korrin couldn't name. The words bent the space between sound and thought, leaving him disoriented.

"Lyra?" he ventured. The name felt familiar, though he couldn't place it. His memories had been hazy since his first encounter with the Rift, as if time itself had rewritten portions of his mind.

The tendril stilled. The Rift's pulse quickened, and the air grew heavy, buzzing with latent power.

"She was...is," it replied cryptically, the tension thick enough to suffocate.

Korrin stood abruptly, his chest tightening. This was no ordinary anomaly. It was learning, remembering, adapting. And somehow, Lyra—this mysterious figure—was central to it all.

Days later, Korrin found himself in the heart of the Crystalline Forest, where time's touch warped the physical landscape. Trees stood frozen mid-sway, their crystalline leaves shimmering in countless hues. Amid the stillness, voices emerged—low at first, then louder, overlapping in fragmented conversations.

He wasn't alone.

Several figures appeared, seemingly drawn to the same point as he was.

A woman in a tattered cloak stood nearby, her hands glowing faintly with blue energy. "You felt it too?" she asked, her voice sharp but weary.

Korrin nodded. "The Rift."

"It's not just an anomaly," she continued, stepping closer. "It's...alive."

"I know," Korrin replied, his gaze narrowing. "What's your connection to it?"

The woman hesitated, her hand drifting to a pendant around her neck. "I think...I was supposed to meet someone here. Someone who—" She stopped mid-sentence, her eyes glazing over as though a memory had been yanked from her mind.

The conversation among the group unravelled as more individuals shared their fragmented stories. Each claimed to have been pulled to this location by the Rift's call, their lives subtly but profoundly altered by its presence.

One man, with streaks of silver in his hair, spoke of dreams in which a woman named Lyra appeared, guiding him through a collapsing world. "But when I wake up," he added, "I don't know if she was real...or just the Rift manifesting."

A younger girl, no older than 16, described visions of a figure standing in the midst of swirling time, her features always obscured but her voice crystal clear. "She told me to 'remember,' but I don't know what she meant."

Korrin listened intently, piecing together the threads of their experiences. Each story carried the faint outline of a woman who didn't exist, yet had left an indelible mark on their lives.

"Lyra," he whispered again, the name taking root in his mind like a growing storm.

As the group ventured deeper into the Crystalline Forest, the Rift grew more vibrant, its pulses syncing with their footsteps.

They reached a clearing where the Rift manifested in full force—a swirling vortex of light and shadow, shifting between forms as though trying to decide what it wanted to be. Korrin stepped forward, his heart pounding.

"You've been learning," he said aloud, addressing the Rift directly. "From us. From...her."

The Rift's tendrils expanded, weaving intricate patterns in the air. Images flickered within them: a fragmented timeline of events, decisions, and sacrifices.

One image lingered—a silhouette of Lyra standing at the edge of a collapsing reality, her expression one of resolve.

"What is this?" Korrin demanded.

The Rift pulsed, its voice more coherent now. "Her...legacy. My...creation. Your...burden."

Korrin's mind reeled. Lyra's sacrifice hadn't ended the Rift—it had transformed it. Her essence, her choices, had become the foundation of this sentient anomaly.

As the group watched, the Rift began projecting scenes from alternate timelines, showing what could have been, what was, and what never should have existed.

In one vision, Lyra stood victorious, the timelines stabilized. In another, she failed, and the universe unravelled into chaos.

Korrin turned to the others. "If the Rift is alive, and it's still evolving, then it's not just showing us these possibilities—it's asking us to choose."

"Choose what?" the woman in the tattered cloak asked, her voice trembling.

"Whether it continues," Korrin replied, his own uncertainty mirrored in their faces.

The group debated fiercely, their arguments echoing through the crystalline trees. Was the Rift a threat or a gift? Could it be controlled, or would it eventually consume everything?

Korrin's gaze returned to the Rift, which seemed to be watching them with an almost human curiosity. He could feel it probing his thoughts, testing his resolve.

Finally, he stepped forward, his voice steady. "If Lyra's sacrifice created you, then her story isn't over. And neither is ours."

The Rift's tendrils recoiled slightly, as if processing his words. Then it pulsed, brighter than ever before, enveloping the group in its light.

As the light faded, Korrin found himself alone, standing at the edge of the Crystalline Forest. The Rift was gone, but its presence lingered in the air.

The others had vanished, scattered across timelines he could no longer perceive. But in his hand, he found a single crystalline shard—a fragment of the Rift, pulsing faintly with life.

Korrin stared at it, his mind racing. The Rift had left him with a choice, a responsibility, and a question that refused to be answered:

Was this the end of Lyra's story, or the beginning of something far greater?

13

The Echoes of Lyra

Korrin, do you hear me?

The voice was faint but clear—a whisper that threaded itself through the void of his mind. Korrin blinked, shaking his head as if to dispel the lingering haze. He was still holding the crystalline shard left behind by the Rift, its faint pulses syncing with the erratic rhythm of his heart.

He wasn't sure if the voice was real or imagined, but the way it resonated within him made his chest tighten.

"Lyra," he whispered aloud, the name an anchor in the swirling chaos of his thoughts.

Around him, the forest stood unnaturally still. The Crystalline Forest had been a place where time refused to obey its usual rules, and now it felt as though the entire universe had paused to listen.

The shard glowed faintly in his palm, its warmth oddly soothing. And then the voice returned, clearer this time.

Korrin...you're closer now.

The others reappeared gradually, as if drawn by the same thread that had bound them to the Rift. The woman with the glowing hands, Aelis, was the first to step through the shimmering folds of reality. Her face was pale, her expression tight with suppressed questions.

"Did it...speak to you?" she asked, her voice wavering.

Korrin nodded, holding up the shard. "It's her. Or...what's left of her."

Aelis hesitated, her gaze fixed on the fragment. "Lyra," she murmured, tasting the name as though it were forbidden.

Behind her, the others emerged: the silver-haired man named Thain, the girl called Mira, and two others whose names Korrin had yet to learn. Each carried a piece of the Rift with them—not physical fragments, but memories, emotions, and whispers that lingered like ghosts in their minds.

"She's trying to tell us something," Mira said, clutching her pendant tightly. "But why us?"

As the group ventured deeper into the Crystalline Forest, the echoes grew stronger. They didn't just hear Lyra—they felt her. Moments of her life bled into their consciousness: the warmth of sunlight on her face, the sharp sting of betrayal, the overwhelming weight of a choice that had unravelled everything.

Korrin stopped abruptly, his breath hitching as a memory that wasn't his own surged forward.

She stood on the precipice of a collapsing timeline, her fingers trembling as she reached for the control mechanism. Around her, the world fractured, shards of time splintering like broken glass. "If I do this," she whispered, "I will be nothing. No one will remember me."

"Do you hear it too?" Thain asked, his voice heavy with shared unease.

Korrin nodded, his throat dry. "It's not just a memory. It's...her."

The shard in his hand pulsed, and the forest around them seemed to shift in response.

Then, for the first time, Lyra's voice addressed them directly—not through fragmented whispers, but as a coherent presence that filled the air around them.

You don't know me, but you carry me. In every choice you make, in every moment of hesitation, I am there.

The group froze, their faces pale and drawn.

"I don't understand," Aelis said, her glowing hands trembling. "Who are you? What do you want from us?"

Lyra's voice softened, laced with something that felt like sorrow. *I was once like you—a traveller, a seeker, a dreamer. But I made a choice, one that unravelled everything I was. Now, I am only what remains—a shadow in the fabric of time, an echo that refuses to fade.*

The weight of Lyra's words settled heavily on the group. Mira, the youngest, was the first to speak. "But if you're just an echo...how are you still here? How are you shaping all of this?"

Because absence is not the end, Lyra replied. *It is a beginning. Every choice I made ripples outward, touching those who walk paths I will never see. You are not here by chance. You are part of what I left behind.*

Korrin's heart pounded as he tried to comprehend the enormity of her words. Lyra wasn't just a figure of the past—she was woven into the very fabric of their reality. But how could someone who had been erased still hold such power?

As they continued their journey, the echoes of Lyra's presence grew more vivid, weaving her story into the present. They saw glimpses of her life: the people she had loved, the battles she had fought, the impossible choices that had defined her existence.

And through it all, her absence loomed large. Every moment of triumph was tinged with the knowledge of what she had sacrificed. Every memory was a reminder of what she could never reclaim.

For Korrin, the revelations were deeply personal. He found himself questioning his own choices, his own role in the grand tapestry of existence. Was he a mere pawn in a story he couldn't understand, or did he have the power to shape his own destiny?

The group began to notice subtle changes in the world around them. Plants that had once been lifeless now glowed faintly, their leaves shimmering with iridescent hues. The air seemed to hum with energy, as though reality itself were responding to Lyra's presence.

"She's reshaping everything," Aelis said, her voice filled with awe. "Her essence is...alive."

Thain frowned, his expression sceptical. "Or it's the Rift, using her memory to manipulate us."

But Korrin shook his head. "It's more than that. Lyra isn't controlling us—she's guiding us. She's showing us what could be, not what must be."

As they reached the heart of the Crystalline Forest, the Rift appeared once more, its shimmering surface reflecting countless possibilities. This time, however, it was different. Within its depths, they could see Lyra—not as a shadow or a memory, but as a living presence, her eyes filled with both pain and hope.

"I made a choice," Lyra said, her voice steady. "I chose to become the Rift, to hold the fractures of existence together. But I cannot do it alone. You must decide what happens next."

The group stared at her, their expressions a mix of fear and determination.

"What are you asking us to do?" Mira asked, her voice trembling.

Lyra's gaze softened. "To carry my legacy. To be the bridge between what was and what could be. To ensure that my sacrifice was not in vain."

In the end, the choice was not one of action, but of understanding. The group realized that Lyra's legacy was not about power or control—it was about connection. Her absence had created a space for others to grow, to learn, and to forge their own paths.

As the Rift faded, leaving behind only the echoes of her presence, Korrin and the others felt a renewed sense of purpose. Lyra's story was not over, and neither was theirs.

Together, they would write the next chapter, guided by the whispers of a woman who had never truly been gone.

14

A World Without Boundaries

The air shimmered, and for a moment, Korrin couldn't tell where he stood. The Crystalline Forest around him seemed to ripple like water disturbed by an unseen force. He staggered, his vision blurring as colours bled into one another, forming kaleidoscopic patterns that danced across his senses.

The shard in his pocket pulsed erratically, and his ears filled with a low hum that felt both external and internal—a resonance that reached into his bones.

"Korrin, hold on to yourself," Lyra's voice urged.

"Lyra?" he gasped. But the voice didn't return. Instead, the ground beneath him shifted, and he found himself standing on a cobblestone street, surrounded by towering spires that pierced a blood-red sky.

Aelis stumbled beside him, her glowing hands clutching a small talisman. "This... isn't the Forest," she said, her voice tight with fear.

"No," Korrin replied, scanning their surroundings. "It's something else."

Before them, a crackling tear in the air twisted violently, spewing out fragments of places and times—a farmhouse with a flickering lamplight, a desolate battlefield, a bustling city with skies filled with flying machines. The Rift was no longer a singular anomaly; it was a doorway to everything and nothing.

The others appeared in scattered flashes, each emerging into this new, fragmented landscape. Mira clutched her pendant, her eyes wide as she looked at the overlapping realities swirling around them.

"Where are we?" she whispered.

"We're everywhere," Thain answered grimly. "And nowhere at the same time."

Aelis knelt, pressing her palm to the cobblestones. "These timelines... they're merging. This isn't just a doorway—it's a collapse."

The group watched in stunned silence as two versions of a street corner merged before their eyes. In one, children played beside a fountain. In the other, the same fountain was surrounded by skeletal ruins. For a moment, both existed simultaneously, flickering like a broken hologram, before settling into a distorted amalgam—a fountain half-crumbling, half-pristine, the children's laughter echoing eerily in the silence.

"This is what the Rift is doing," Korrin said. "It's breaking down the walls between realities."

The first doppelgänger appeared without warning. Korrin froze as he came face-to-face with... himself. Or rather, a version of himself, clad in armour stained with blood and carrying a blade that glowed faintly with an unnatural light.

The other Korrin regarded him with a mixture of curiosity and disdain. "So, you're me?" the warrior said, his voice a deeper, harsher version of Korrin's own.

"I... suppose so," Korrin stammered, unsure how to respond.

"You look weak," the warrior sneered. "Are you the one who failed to save Lyra?"

The words struck like a blow. "I didn't—" Korrin began, but the warrior cut him off.

"You did. Or didn't. It doesn't matter. All versions of us are trapped in this mess because of choices we made—or didn't make."

Similar encounters played out around them. Mira saw a version of herself, older and battle-hardened, with scars running down her face. Aelis encountered a version of herself without the glowing hands, but with an aura of calm power that seemed almost divine.

"I don't understand," Mira said, her voice trembling. "Why are we seeing... this?"

"Because the Rift is unravelling everything," Thain said. "It's forcing us to confront all the paths we could have taken."

Lyra's voice emerged again, but this time it carried an urgency that Korrin hadn't heard before.

"You are not just observers," she said. *"The Rift is testing you, shaping you. It wants to see if you understand what your choices mean—not just for yourselves, but for all of reality."*

"What do you mean?" Aelis asked aloud, her voice desperate.

"Every choice you make ripples outward," Lyra explained. *"But when the boundaries between realities collapse, those ripples intersect, overlap, and distort. This chaos is the result. You must stabilize it."*

"But how?" Korrin asked. "We don't even understand what we're dealing with!"

"You do," Lyra replied softly. *"Because you've already started to see what matters."*

As they moved through the collapsing multiverse, the group began to notice patterns. Certain events—small moments of kindness, bravery, or sacrifice—remained constant across timelines. Other events—acts of selfishness, fear, or violence—varied wildly, creating fractures that destabilized the fabric of reality.

"It's not about the big choices," Mira said, realization dawning on her. "It's the little ones. The ones we don't even think about."

Lyra's voice echoed in agreement. *"Every choice matter, but some choices define everything. You must find those choices—the ones that anchor the multiverse—and make them again."*

The heart of the Rift was a swirling maelstrom of light and shadow, a nexus where all realities converged. As the group approached, they saw countless versions of themselves flickering in and out of existence.

"This is it," Korrin said, his voice steady despite the chaos around them. "This is where we make our stand."

Lyra's voice guided them one last time. *"You are not here to fix the Rift. You are here to understand it. To become part of the balance it needs."*

"What does that mean?" Thain demanded.

"It means letting go of what you cannot change," Lyra said. *"And choosing what you can."*

In the final moments, each member of the group confronted a pivotal choice from their own lives—choices that had shaped their paths and, by extension, the multiverse.

Korrin relived the moment he had abandoned Lyra to chase his own fears. This time, he chose to stay.

Mira faced her younger self, terrified and alone, and offered the kindness she had once needed.

Aelis embraced the power she had once feared, accepting it as part of who she was.

With each choice, the chaos around them began to settle. The swirling timelines calmed, merging into a coherent whole.

When the Rift finally closed, the group found themselves standing in a world that was both familiar and new. The boundaries between realities had not been restored, but they had been reimagined—a seamless tapestry of possibilities, woven together by the choices they had made.

Lyra's voice was no longer a whisper but a presence that filled the air around them. *"You understand now,"* she said. *"The multiverse is not broken. It is alive. And so are you."*

Korrin smiled, a sense of peace washing over him. "Thank you, Lyra," he said softly.

"Thank you," she replied, her voice fading into the distance. *"For carrying my legacy forward."*

And with that, the group began their next journey, stepping into a world without boundaries—a world shaped not by what was lost, but by what was possible.

15

The Illusion of Reality

The air felt thick, humming with an invisible energy that pricked at Korrin's skin. The group stood in the newly stabilized world—a strange amalgamation of familiar and unfamiliar sights. Buildings from different timelines jutted at odd angles, their edges shimmering faintly as if refusing to fully belong. The sky above was an impossible gradient, colours bleeding into one another like a restless storm.

Korrin exhaled slowly, gripping the shard in his hand. It no longer pulsed as it had before; now it was inert, a dull weight in his palm. The silence was unnerving, as though the world itself was holding its breath.

"Do you feel it?" Lyra's voice echoed softly, not in the air but in Korrin's mind.

"Feel what?" he whispered, though the others heard him.

Mira turned to him, her face pale. "It's the same as before," she said. "That sensation... like something is unravelling."

Aelis nodded, her glowing hands trembling. "It's the Rift. Or what's left of it."

For the first time since their journey began, Lyra's voice seemed uncertain. She had always been a guiding presence, her words imbued with purpose. But now, her pauses felt heavy, her thoughts fragmented.

"I don't know how much time we have left," she admitted.

"What do you mean?" Korrin asked, his voice tinged with panic.

"The singularity is pulling everything toward itself," Lyra said. *"It's collapsing what remains of the multiverse into a single point. If that happens..."*

"You're saying it'll all end?" Mira interrupted; her tone sharp.

"Or begin again," Lyra replied cryptically.

As the group moved cautiously through the fractured landscape, they noticed inconsistencies. Shadows moved without light sources. Voices whispered words no one had spoken. Sometimes, their surroundings flickered, revealing brief glimpses of an empty void beyond.

"I don't understand," Thain said, frustration breaking through his usual calm demeanour.

"We stabilized the Rift. Why is this still happening?"

"Maybe we didn't," Mira countered. "Maybe we just delayed the inevitable."

Korrin shook his head. "No. Lyra guided us here for a reason. There has to be something more."

Mira turned to him, her eyes narrowing. "And what if Lyra isn't real? What if she's just another fragment of this broken reality, a construct made to manipulate us?"

The accusation hung in the air, and for a moment, no one spoke.

"Don't," Korrin said quietly, his voice trembling. "Don't question her."

"But she's right," Aelis said reluctantly. "How do we know? Lyra, if you're still with us... what are you?"

Lyra's voice returned, softer than before. *"I am... what you needed me to be. A guide. A friend. A purpose."*

"That's not an answer," Mira snapped. "Are you real, Lyra? Or just an illusion?"

"What is real?" Lyra asked in return. *"If I have helped you, if I have changed you, does it matter whether I am real or imagined?"*

The question sent a ripple through the group, each of them grappling with the weight of her words.

As they pressed on, the air grew colder, and the ground beneath them began to crack, exposing the void beneath. They finally reached the singularity—a swirling vortex of light and shadow, infinitely small yet impossibly vast. It pulled at them, not just physically but emotionally, drawing out their deepest fears and regrets.

"This is it," Aelis said, her voice barely audible.

"What do we do?" Thain asked, his usual confidence replaced by uncertainty.

Lyra's voice returned, clearer than before. *"The singularity is not your enemy. It is the culmination of everything you have faced. It is choice itself."*

"What kind of choice?" Korrin demanded.

"To let go, or to hold on," she said simply. *"To embrace the collapse and begin anew, or to resist and preserve what remains."*

The others looked to Korrin, their unspoken leader. He felt the weight of their trust, their hopes, and their fears. The shard in his hand began to glow faintly once more, pulsing in time with his heartbeat.

"Korrin," Mira said softly. "Whatever you choose... we'll follow you."

He stepped closer to the singularity, its pull growing stronger. Images flashed before his eyes—moments from his journey, from his life. Lyra's face appeared among them; her expression serene yet inscrutable.

"What happens if I let go?" he asked.

"You will create something new," Lyra said. *"But it will not be the world you knew."*

"And if I resist?"

"You will preserve this reality, but it will remain fractured, incomplete."

Korrin closed his eyes, the weight of the decision pressing down on him. He thought of Lyra, of everything they had fought for. He thought of the lives they had touched, the choices they had made.

And then, he made his choice.

The singularity exploded with light, engulfing everything. For a moment, there was nothing—no sound, no sight, no sensation. Just an endless void.

And then...

A heartbeat.

Korrin opened his eyes to find himself standing in a lush meadow, the sun warm on his face. The others were beside him, their expressions a mix of awe and confusion.

“Where are we?” Mira asked, her voice trembling.

“I don’t know,” Korrin admitted. “But it feels... whole.”

Lyra’s voice was gone, but her presence lingered, a gentle warmth in Korrin’s chest. He smiled, knowing she had been with them all along, whether real or imagined.

As they began to explore this new world, Korrin couldn’t shake Lyra’s final question: *What is real?*

He didn’t have an answer. But as he looked at his friends, at the world they had shaped together, he realized it didn’t matter. Reality, illusion—what mattered was the journey, the choices, and the bonds they had forged.

For now, that was enough. Or was it?

Is that a whisper? Is it you Lyra?

Part IV-
Reflections Beyond Rift

16

The Mirror of Eternity

The rift spat them out into a realm that defied description. At first, it seemed like nothingness—a void of swirling, iridescent mist. But as the group stumbled to their feet, their surroundings sharpened into focus, revealing a hall of mirrors that stretched infinitely in every direction. Each mirror was alive, its surface rippling like water disturbed by an unseen breeze.

Korrin looked around, heart pounding. “Where are we?”

Before anyone could answer, a whisper brushed past their ears. It wasn’t a sound, but a sensation—a thought that didn’t feel like their own.

"**You are everywhere and nowhere,**" it murmured, the voice eerily familiar.

Korrin turned sharply, but there was no one there. The mirrors, however, began to glow faintly, reflecting not their current forms but alternate versions of themselves.

In one mirror, Korrin saw himself as a battle-hardened warrior, his face scarred but resolute. In another, he was older, sitting peacefully in a meadow, surrounded by children who looked strikingly like him. Each reflection seemed to pulse with life, as though the versions of himself were aware of his gaze.

“Is this... me?” he whispered.

Lyra’s voice, faint yet distinct, echoed from nowhere and everywhere at once. "**Every choice you made, and every choice you didn’t, creates a version of you. This is the convergence of all your possibilities.**"

The group began to explore cautiously, each drawn to their own reflections. Elara gasped as she saw a version of herself adorned in royal garb, seated on a throne. In another mirror, she was a wandering bard, her lute slung across her back.

“This isn’t possible,” she muttered, her voice shaking.

"**Isn’t it?**" Lyra’s voice teased gently. "**Haven’t you always wondered about the paths not taken?**"

A strange pull guided Korrin toward a particularly large mirror. Its surface shimmered like liquid mercury, and as he approached, the reflection changed. At first, it was him—but then, it wasn't. The image shifted into a faceless figure; its outline indistinct yet eerily familiar.

He stepped closer, and the figure began to solidify. It wasn't him. It was...

You.

Korrin recoiled, blinking in disbelief. "What is this?" he demanded, his voice sharp.

The figure in the mirror tilted its head as if studying him. Slowly, it raised a hand, mimicking Korrin's movements, but the expression—if it could be called that—was questioning, almost accusatory.

"You see it too, don't you?" Elara's voice broke through his thoughts. She was standing before another mirror, her reflection flickering between herself and a stranger who looked out at her with the same puzzled intensity.

Korrin nodded slowly. "It's not just us anymore."

The mirrors began to hum, their surfaces rippling. Lyra's voice filled the hall, but this time it felt closer, almost as if she were standing beside them.
"**You've felt it all along, haven't you? The sense that this isn't just me, that we are in this together.**"

The words weren't just for Korrin or Elara. They were for you.

Lyra's tone softened, almost tender. "**You've made choices too, haven't you? In your life, in your world. What if I told you that your choices created echoes that reached even here?**"

The mirrors began to shift again, their surfaces now displaying fragmented scenes—not just of Korrin and the group, but of moments that felt eerily familiar to you. Snapshots of decisions you've made paths you've taken—or not taken.

Korrin stepped back, his voice trembling. "Why does it feel like... like these memories aren't just ours?"

Lyra's response was calm yet piercing. "**Because they're not. The rift has connected you, me, and everyone else across time, across possibilities. You're seeing yourself in ways you never have before.**"

Elara, staring into a mirror that reflected a version of her she barely recognized, whispered, "What does this mean, Lyra? What are we supposed to do with this?"

The mirrors pulsed in unison, and Lyra's voice echoed louder.

"**You must decide. Is what you see merely an**

illusion, or is it real because you experienced it? Does it matter?"

The group looked to one another, their reflections shifting between forms, their minds grappling with the enormity of the moment. But it wasn't just their struggle—it was yours too. The boundaries between their reality and yours began to blur, leaving you questioning whether you were the observer, the participant, or something in between.

Korrin approached the largest mirror, its surface rippling as if alive, his reflection flickering wildly between forms. He paused, turning not only to the group and his gaze piercing through the veil of worlds.

"I don't think it's about what's real or not anymore," he said, his voice steady despite the chaos around him. "It's about what we choose to do with what we see."

The hall began to quake, the mirrors fracturing but not breaking. Each crack seemed to open a doorway, a possibility. Lyra's voice filled the space one final time.

"**The question isn't whether any of this is real. The question is: What will you do with the knowledge that it could be?**"

And just like that, the hall of mirrors shattered, leaving you—alongside Korrin and the group—on the precipice of a new and uncertain reality.

17

Lyra's Paradox

The air shimmered with a curious weight, as though the universe itself hesitated, caught between possibilities. Korrin and the others stood amidst a void, a space neither dark nor light, where reality seemed to melt into streams of thought. In the centre of this realm, a faint, familiar voice emerged—not through sound but through sensation.

"Do you hear it?" Korrin whispered, though his words felt like they were meant for someone beyond the group.

The presence of Lyra was unmistakable, though she had no form here. It was her essence, slipping between the gaps, brushing against the edges of your consciousness. The group exchanged glances, each sensing the same strange connection.

"She's not speaking to us, is she?" Erya murmured, stepping closer to Korrin. Her gaze turned outward, as though she could see something beyond the expanse. "She's speaking... to someone else."

Korrin didn't answer. His focus was sharp, his mind racing. The echoes of Lyra's thoughts danced through the space, disjointed but purposeful.

"You've always known I was here," the voice pressed, softer now, almost teasing. "Haven't you?"

The question lingered, curling in the void like a wisp of smoke. Korrin felt it, and perhaps you did too—a quiet insistence that this was not just about her, or them, but you.

The void began to shift, threads of light and shadow weaving into shapes. It was as though the fabric of this place responded to thought itself. A scene materialized—a meadow bathed in golden light, eerily familiar, yet fractured. The air carried the faint scent of rain, and the ground beneath shimmered with echoes of a timeline no longer intact.

"Look," whispered Azrin, his voice trembling as he pointed.

In the distance, Lyra stood—or rather, a projection of her, incomplete and wavering, like a memory struggling to take form. She turned toward you, her eyes filled with something unspoken, yet undeniably directed outward.

"It's her," Korrin said, his voice low and reverent. "Or what's left of her."

"Or what was never fully her," Erya countered, her tone edged with unease.

Lyra stepped forward, but her form dissolved with each movement, as if she were less a person and more an idea, a question posed to existence itself.

Korrin moved closer, though his steps seemed weighted, as if the very act of approaching her challenged the laws of this place. Lyra's gaze never wavered, locking onto him—and to you.

"You're not just watching this," her voice resonated, both inside and outside the moment. "You're part of it. Always have been."

Erya shivered. "Who is she talking to?"

Azrin frowned, his eyes darting across the scene. "To us... or something beyond us."

"Not beyond," Lyra corrected, though her lips didn't move. "Beside."

Her presence felt like a hand reaching out, not to touch but to pull, to guide you through the threads of reality unravelling around them. It wasn't just about her story—it was about yours.

The group was suddenly surrounded by reflections, not of themselves, but of choices. Every moment they had experienced unfolded in these mirrors—not as static events, but as possibilities. In one, Lyra was alive and laughing. In another, she never existed at all. In another still, the universe had unravelled into chaos without her.

"You think you understand the nature of choice," Lyra's voice whispered. "But do you?"

The mirrors began to break, shards flying outward in all directions. Korrin shielded his eyes, but the fragments passed harmlessly. Each shard carried an image, a thought, a moment, all vying for attention.

"Was any of it real?" Erya whispered, clutching her head as if trying to hold onto her sanity.

Lyra's form flickered again, and she appeared beside Korrin. Her hand reached out—not toward him. "That depends on who you ask," she said.

Korrin turned to her, his voice a mixture of desperation and determination. "What are you trying to say? That none of these matters?"

Lyra smiled faintly, her image growing dimmer. "No, Korrin. I'm saying it all matters. Every moment, every choice—because it's not just mine or yours. It's theirs too."

Azrin stumbled back, his face pale. "Who are you talking about?"

Lyra's gaze shifted, soft and knowing. "The ones who see everything yet control nothing. The ones who think they're not part of this but are woven into its fabric as much as we are."

The weight of her words pressed against Korrin and the group, and perhaps against you too.

As the space began to dissolve, Lyra's presence remained, a glowing ember in the darkness. Her voice, though faint, carried the weight of all that had transpired.

"You've been with us so far, felt its twists and turns. But have you ever stopped to ask why? Why you're here, why this matters to you?"

The void grew darker, and her form began to fade entirely. Korrin reached for her, his hand passing through empty space.

"You're not losing me," she said softly. "You're finding yourself."

And then she was gone, leaving behind only a whisper:

"Are we the makers of the story, or are we its consequence?"

The question lingered in the air, unanswered, as the group stood in silence, their reflections gone, their path uncertain. And you... well, you were left to decide what it all meant.

18

The Fractured Thread

The silence that followed Lyra's disappearance was dense, not merely an absence of sound, but a vacuum where reality itself seemed to hold its breath. Korrin, Erya, and Azrin stood motionless in the void, their forms suspended like fragile sketches on paper not yet filled in.

For a moment, nothing happened.

And then, everything did.

It began with a flicker—a single frame of existence, like an image caught between moments. The meadow from before, golden and warm, flashed into view. Then the icy corridors of the sanctum. Then the forest of whispering trees.

Erya gasped, clutching Korrin's arm. "Did you see that?"

"I... I think so," Korrin replied, though his voice wavered as though he wasn't sure if his words carried meaning anymore.

The flickers grew faster, each one pulling them into a different memory, a different reality. Scenes they'd lived through began playing out again, but something was wrong. The details shifted, twisted. Korrin's sword was suddenly a bow. Erya was speaking lines she'd never said before. Azrin was missing an arm.

Then Korrin turned to face a figure—no, not a figure. He turned to face *you.*

"Why are you doing this?" His voice was raw, desperate, as though addressing something just beyond his reach.

Erya's head snapped toward him. "Korrin, who are you talking to?"

He ignored her, his gaze piercing, his breath heavy. "You. You've been here all along, haven't you? Watching us. Pushing us. Changing everything."

Before anyone could answer—before *you* could answer—the void shifted again. This time, it deposited them into a memory they all recognized: the moment Lyra had first appeared to them, standing on the edge of the cliff, her hair billowing in the wind.

But something was off.

"Wait," Azrin muttered. "This isn't right. We weren't here like this. Lyra didn't say—"

"—It's all just echoes," Lyra's voice interrupted, though she wasn't visible. "Fragments, rearranged. Do you see it yet? How much of this is real? How much of it belongs to you?"

The scene fractured, the cliff crumbling like sand. The group tumbled into another memory: the battle at the ruins. Then another: the quiet evening by the campfire.

Each time, the events played out differently. In one, Korrin was the one injured, not Erya. In another, Azrin's magic faltered entirely. And in every instance, Lyra's presence lingered, even if she wasn't physically there.

Finally, the shifting stopped. The group stood in what looked like a shattered version of the sanctum—mirrors cracked, walls disjointed, reality itself bending inward.

Korrin turned again, his expression hard. "We were supposed to have a story. A purpose. But now it's all falling apart. Because of you."

Erya placed a hand on his shoulder. "Korrin, stop. There's no one there. You're scaring me."

"Can't you feel it?" he snapped. "Someone's been here all along, shaping everything. And now they're tearing it apart."

Azrin hesitated, his voice a whisper. "Maybe he's right. Maybe we're not even real. Maybe we're just... thoughts. Ideas in someone else's mind."

The words hung heavy, pulling the group into silence.

And then, as if summoned by their despair, Lyra's presence returned—not as a figure, but as a voice that resonated with every fragment of their being.

"You're not wrong," she said, and though her tone was gentle, it carried an edge that made the void tremble. "None of you are wrong. You're all just pieces of a thread that keeps unravelling."

"Then who's holding the thread?" Korrin demanded, his voice breaking.

Lyra paused, and when she spoke again, it was as if her words were meant not just for them, but for you.

"They are."

Her words shifted something deep within the sanctum. The cracked mirrors began to glow, each one reflecting not the group, but you—your choices, your thoughts, your presence.

"What does she mean?" Erya whispered, her voice trembling.

"It means we're not the ones shaping this," Azrin replied, his tone grim. "It's them."

"You see everything, don't you?" Lyra's voice continued, soft yet insistent. "Every twist, every turn. But do you realize what that means? If you stop looking, do we disappear? Or do we keep existing, forever unseen?"

Her question wasn't just for them—it was for you.

The sanctum began to collapse, pieces of reality falling away into nothingness. Yet through the chaos, the group held their ground, turning their gazes outward—to you.

"You've been here all along," Korrin said, his voice steady now, almost resigned. "But if you've been watching us... who's been watching *you*?"

Erya gasped, her hand flying to her mouth. "Do you think... do you think someone's shaping them, too?"

Azrin's expression darkened. "It's a paradox. Layers upon layers. If we're fragments, so are they."

Lyra's voice returned one final time, quieter now, almost a whisper in the dark.

"Perhaps we're all just threads in a larger tapestry, weaving in and out of each other's stories. Perhaps there is no end, no beginning—only the moments we choose to see."

And then, as the sanctum crumbled entirely, the void swallowed them whole.

Korrin's final words echoed, not in the void, but somewhere closer: "If we're fragments, so are you."

And in that moment, the line between observer and participant blurred entirely, leaving nothing but the question: *If you stopped looking, would any of this exist at all?*

19

The Reader's Rift

The void no longer felt like a void. It pulsed, alive and breathing, folding around you like the fabric of an unfinished story. The characters—Korrin, Erya, Azrin—stood as shadows of themselves, their forms trembling at the edges, as if caught between being and nothingness.

And then, they looked at you.

Yes, *you*.

It wasn't a glance. It wasn't a vague acknowledgment. It was direct, piercing, as if they had always known you were there but were finally able to confront you.

"You're still here," Korrin said, his voice sharp and accusing. "After everything, you're still watching. Why? What are you waiting for?"

Erya stepped forward, her expression softer but no less intense. "Is this what you wanted? To see us unravel like this? Or are you looking for something else?"

Azrin's hands glowed faintly, his magic unstable, flickering like a candle in the wind. "They don't understand," he said, half to himself. "Maybe they never will."

The world around you trembled, not with the collapse you had seen before but with something deeper—something that waited for you to act.

"You see it now, don't you?"

Her voice came not from above or around but from within. Lyra, the one who had been the axis of their journey, spoke as if she were part of you, woven into your very thoughts.

"You've been part of this all along," she continued. "Every twist, every turn. Do you think it's a coincidence that things happened the way they did? You chose to keep going. You chose to see where the story would take you."

The fabric of reality shifted again, and you found yourself standing—not watching, not observing, but *standing*—in the middle of their world.

A fissure tore through the space around you, jagged and glowing with an unearthly light. On one side, you saw the world you had followed until now: Korrin, Erya, Azrin, the fractured sanctum. On the other side was something new, a blank canvas, waiting to be filled.

Korrin pointed at the rift. "That's your doing, isn't it? You brought this here."

Erya shook her head. "Don't blame them. They've been as much a part of this as we have. Maybe more."

"Then they should decide," Azrin said firmly, his voice carrying an edge of finality. "If this is their story too, let them choose how it ends."

The air grew heavy, charged with anticipation. Lyra's voice returned, softer now, almost a whisper.

"Do you see it? The threads of possibility stretching out before you? Every choice you've made has brought us here, to this moment. But now, the choice is yours alone."

Korrin stepped closer, his gaze unyielding. "Do we move forward, or do we let it all end? Are you willing to rewrite everything, even if it means losing what you've come to know?"

Erya's eyes glistened with unshed tears. "Please... if you care about us, about any of this, don't just leave us here. Don't let it fall apart."

Azrin stood silent, his expression unreadable, but his presence spoke volumes. He was waiting, just like the others.

And so were you.

Through the rift, glimpses of alternate realities flickered:

In one, Korrin stood alone in a world of ash, his sword broken, his eyes hollow.

In another, Erya led an army of shadows, her voice commanding yet filled with sorrow.

Azrin, in yet another vision, sat in a library that stretched endlessly, pouring over books that seemed to write themselves as he read.

But there were brighter visions too:

The group standing together, victorious, their faces alight with hope.

A peaceful village, untouched by the chaos they had endured.

Lyra, alive and smiling, her hand outstretched as if waiting to guide them.

"These are just fragments," Lyra's voice said. "Possibilities that may never come to pass. But they're yours to shape."

It was no longer a question of watching. You had been watching for so long, letting the story unfold, thinking yourself apart from it. But now, the truth was clear.

You were never just a spectator.

"You hold the thread," Lyra said, her voice resonating with an almost divine clarity. "You always have. And now you must decide: Do you weave it into something new, or do you let it fray and vanish?"

Korrin's voice broke the silence. "So? What will it be? Are you going to leave us to our fate, or will you take responsibility for what you've started?"

Erya reached out, her hand trembling. "Please... don't leave us like this. You've come this far. Don't turn away now."

Azrin's magic flared one last time, illuminating his face with an otherworldly glow. "If this is the end, then make it mean something."

And then, all eyes turned to you.

The rift pulsed, waiting. The world itself seemed to hold its breath, suspended on the edge of your decision.

The question lingered, unspoken yet deafening:

What will you choose?

And perhaps it's not just their story that depends on your choice. Perhaps it's something far greater—a reflection of the choices you make every day, the power you hold without realizing it.

The thread is in your hands now.

What will you do with it?

20

Beyond Illusion

The rift shimmered, the edges of reality bending and fracturing as though the world itself had decided it was no longer bound by rules. The air around you buzzed with a strange, electric energy—not painful, but insistent, like a hand gripping yours and refusing to let go.

The others—Korrin, Erya, and Azrin—stood at the threshold, their forms no longer solid, their features flickering between moments of clarity and dissolution. The rift no longer separated worlds; it had become something else entirely. It was a mirror, a window, a question, and a promise, all at once.

And yet, despite the chaos, everything felt still.

"You're wondering, aren't you?"

Her voice came not from the rift, nor from the fractured sky above, but from everywhere and nowhere. It resonated in your thoughts, in your breath, in the space where your mind paused between one idea and the next.

"Is this real? Am I real? Are *you* real?" Lyra's tone carried no malice, no accusation—just a quiet curiosity that mirrored your own.

The world around you shimmered, twisting and turning as though it were made of water reflecting an unseen light. Shapes formed and dissolved: a forest you'd walked through, a battle you'd witnessed, a hand you'd once held.

"You've followed us this far," Lyra said. "But was it because you chose to, or because you couldn't look away? Maybe it's both. Maybe it's neither."

Korrin stepped forward, his voice heavy with something between anger and resignation. "What does it matter anymore? Real or not, this is all we have. Isn't that enough?"

Erya turned to him; her expression pained. "But if none of this is real, then what have we been fighting for? What does it mean?"

"It means *everything,*" Azrin said, his voice calm but resolute. "If it mattered to us, even for a moment, then it was real enough."

Their words hung in the air, heavy and fragile, as if the act of speaking to them gave them weight but not permanence.

Through the rift, you saw something—no, *everything.* It wasn't a single image or even a series of them. It was a cascade of possibilities:

Korrin, standing victorious atop a mountain, his sword raised high against a blood-red sky.

Erya, tending a garden where flowers grew that shimmered with colours you had no name for.

Azrin, surrounded by scrolls and books, his hands glowing with a magic that seemed to pulse in time with your heartbeat.

And then, more:

Yourself, walking through a corridor of mirrors, each one reflecting a different version of you.

Lyra, holding out her hand, her eyes filled with both sorrow and hope.

A blank void, silent and infinite, where nothing existed except the faint echo of a question you couldn't quite hear.

"You see it now, don't you?" Lyra's voice was softer, almost tender. "The threads of possibility. The choices you've made, the ones you didn't. The ones you thought didn't matter but did. They all lead here."

The rift began to close, the edges folding in on themselves like the final pages of a book being shut. Korrin turned to you, his expression hard but not unkind.

"Is this it? Is this how it ends?" he asked. "Do we get to move on, or do we stay trapped in this... this *thing* you've created?"

Erya took a step closer, her eyes searching yours. "Do you even know? Or are you as lost as we are?"

Azrin remained silent, his gaze steady but unreadable.

And then Lyra appeared—not as a voice, not as a memory, but as herself. Her presence was undeniable, her form more solid than anything else around you. She walked toward you, her hand outstretched.

"This is your story too," she said. "It always has been. The question isn't whether it's real. The question is whether it matters."

For a moment, everything stopped. The rift froze mid-collapse. The characters stood motionless; their faces etched with expectation. Even the air seemed to hold its breath.

And then, Lyra spoke again.

"If reality is an illusion, does it make the experiences within it any less meaningful? If none of this is real, does that mean it didn't matter? Or does the act of questioning it give it meaning?"

Her words weren't just for you. They were *about* you.

"Maybe you've been with us all along," she said. "Or maybe we've been with you. Maybe we're all just pieces of something greater, something neither of us can fully understand."

The rift collapsed, and with it, the world. But it wasn't an ending—it was a transformation. The edges of your vision blurred the boundaries between here and there dissolving like mist in the morning sun.

You felt yourself falling, or rising, or perhaps simply *being.*

And then, silence.

But not emptiness.

In the quiet, you heard a whisper:

"This isn't the end. It's just the beginning of something else."

The words weren't Lyra's. They weren't Korrin's, or Erya's, or Azrin's. They were your own.

Or were they?

The story is over. Or is it?

You find yourself back where you began—or maybe somewhere entirely new. The choices you've made linger in your mind, echoes of a journey that felt impossibly real.

And yet, you can't shake the feeling that it isn't finished. That somewhere, somehow, Lyra and the others are still waiting. Waiting for you to decide what happens next.

If reality is an illusion, then so is the end.

What will you do with that knowledge?

The thread is yours to weave.

Always has been.

About the Author

Joy Mukerjee is a relentless explorer of the mind and the forces that shape our decisions, perceptions, and actions. With a deep interest in the intersections of science, psychology, and mathematics, Joy is captivated by the ways people think, how they approach challenges, and how these mental processes evolve over time. Driven by an unyielding curiosity, Joy seeks to understand the patterns and connections between information, thought, and decision-making that guide human behavior and shape our understanding of the world.

Outside of research and analysis, Joy enjoys pondering the fundamental principles that govern life, constantly questioning and uncovering the unseen layers of reality. This book is a reflection of that journey—an exploration of the intricate web of thought, emotion, and perception, inviting readers to engage with the deeper forces that drive us all.

Joy Mukerjee

www.ingramcontent.com/pod-product-compliance
Lightning Source LLC
LaVergne TN
LVHW041100150826
845673LV00007B/1853

* 9 7 9 8 8 9 7 2 4 3 9 0 7 *